W9-BJS-215

JUN 2010

TWENTY
GOLD FALCONS

Also by Amy Gordon

Magic by Heart

Return to Gill Park

The Secret Life of a Boarding School Brat

The Gorillas of Gill Park

AMY GORDON

Holiday House / New York

The publisher would like to thank Bruna Charifker
of New York University for reviewing the Portuguese
in this book for accuracy.

Text copyright © 2010 by Amy Gordon
All Right Reserved
HOLIDAY HOUSE is registered in the U.S. Patent and Trademark Office.
Printed and bound in February 2010 at Worzalla, Stevens Point, WI, USA.
www.holidayhouse.com
First Edition
1 3 5 7 9 10 8 6 4 2

Library of Congress Cataloging-in-Publication Data
Gordon, Amy, 1949-
Twenty gold falcons / by Amy Gordon.—1st ed.
p. cm.
Summary: Twelve-year-old Aiden is very unhappy when, after her father's
death, her mother moves them from the family farm, but soon she and new
friends are caught up in the search for long-lost coins in the historic Ingle
building that towers over the city of Gloria.
ISBN 978-0-8234-2252-4 (hardcover)
[1. Historic buildings—Fiction.   2. Moving, Household—Fiction.   3. City
and town life—Fiction.   4. Coins—Fiction.   5. Peregrine falcon—Fiction.
6. Falcons—Fiction.   7. Schools—Fiction.]   I. Title.
PZ7.G65Twe 2010
[Fic]—dc22
2009046499

For Tim

I suddenly had that hold-your-breath feeling I'd had as a little kid. Mom, my uncle Tony, and I stood in the little hallway in the east wing of the Ingle Building waiting in front of the brass doors for an elevator. I hadn't been there for more than a year, but I had always loved that moment when the doors to elevator number one opened.

Bing, and a second later there was Rosie, the elevator operator, just as I remembered her, roly-poly and cheerful, a bundle of pink knitting in her lap. The little space she was in glowed with the light of a gently swaying crystal chandelier that hung from the center of the ceiling.

"Oh, my dollings," Rosie said, turning to us immediately. She put her knitting down and stood and wrapped her arms around Mom. "Tony told me—I'm so sorry about your loss, Allegra; so young to lose your husband, so sad. But you're doing the right thing, moving back home to Gloria!"

My mom and my uncle Tony had been born and raised in Gloria, but I had grown up on a farm way upstate and had only been to Gloria maybe four times in my life. *This is not my home*, I wanted to say, tears springing into my eyes.

Rosie turned and hugged me, too. "My word, Aiden, I think you've grown a foot since the last time I saw you. How old are you now?"

"Twelve," I mumbled.

"Marvelous age!" Rosie exclaimed. Then she pointed to my head. "That cap you're wearing, dolling, brings to mind the good old days, it does."

I touched the old, "newsie" style wool hat that Pops had always worn. Mom sighed. "Herb pulled that hat out of our attic one day and wore it all the time, and now Aiden practically wears it to bed." Mom didn't like me wearing it because it was so old and ratty and came down over my eyes.

"Well, I think it suits you, dolling," said Rosie with a quick smile. "And where can I take you folks today?"

"Rooftop, please," said Uncle Tony. "We're here to see the view."

"Rooftop it is," said Rosie. She pressed one of the million brass buttons that took up a good part of the wall next to the doors and then sat back down and took up her knitting again. "That cap does brings to mind your great-grandpa, Fortunato Balboni, Aiden. You never knew him, I expect, but he was a fine old gent. Such a hard worker, he was, arranging all the musical events here in the old days. But he knew how to have a good time, too. He and Mr. Ingle—good friends they became, you know—the two of 'em would dream up such fun things for all the kids growing up here to do. There was a little gang of 'em at the time—my own two, and the Ingle children, and various others—and Mr. Balboni and Mr. Ingle would set 'em on treasure hunts all over the building!" Rosie's face glowed with the memory. "I can still see those children racing all over the place chasing after clues."

"Oh yes," said Mom. "And one time wasn't the treasure gold coins—what were they called? Gold Falcons?"

Rosie nodded. "Not worth much after the Depression, but lovely gold coins they were. That was the hunt the children went on for days and days—it was very elaborate, let me tell you. But Mr. Ingle died unexpectedly before the treasure was ever found, and everyone forgot about the hunt, and the clues got lost. To this day, there are Gold Falcons in this building that have never been found!"

"Now that Aiden's living here in Gloria, she can find the lost gold of the Ingle Building," Tony joked. "Remember, Allie, how we used to look for it?"

"Might be more difficult these days," said Rosie. "We've got a manager now who doesn't like to have kids running about the place." She lowered her voice. "I don't know why Mrs. Ingle put Grip in charge, Tony, I really don't. You know what he's like."

She and Tony were good friends because Tony sang at the Opera House in the Ingle Building. She might have said more, but we had reached the top. "Well, here we are, folks, we have reached our destination!"

As we came out onto the rooftop, Tony led us over to the railing. He handed a pair of binoculars to Mom and spread his arms wide. "There it is, Allegra and Aiden, the glorious city of Gloria! Welcome home!"

"Yes, there it is. It's all still here," said Mom. "I can even see cousin Mitch's tree house. Come look, Aiden. Remember going to the tree house?"

"What do you think, Aiden?" Tony asked. "Do you think you're going to like it here?"

"It'll be great," I said flatly, but as I looked out at all

the streets and buildings, with only the patch of green park in the middle, all I could think about was how much I missed the cow pastures and the barn, my favorite maple tree, and the stone wall where my best friend, Blake, and I kept feathers in a secret place.

I turned my back on the view and looked up at the pink granite mountain peak that rose up from the top of the middle rectangle that formed the Ingle Building. Plunked on that peak was a huge, gold falcon, its wings outstretched as if it were about to take off.

"There are two *real* falcons living up at the top of this building, you know," said Tony. "Lord and Lady Peregrine."

"What?" I turned to look at him, amazed.

"Sure," he said. "Falcons in the wild live on high cliffs, which is why, when they become city dwellers, they take to bridges and high buildings. These two are famous. The pair of them live way up there with Mrs. Ingle. Eighty-seven stories high or something like that. Hey, look—someone's up there on the balcony now. Yep, there's the old dame herself," he said, taking the binoculars.

Mom stood still, looking up at the balcony for a long time. "Sad," she said finally.

"Why sad?" I asked.

"Mr. Ingle died when she was still quite a young woman, and then later she fought with her children and they moved away and never returned, and now—well, she's old and all alone."

I suddenly felt panicky. Mom and I had been fighting a lot lately.

But just as I was turning away, Tony cried out, "There's one of the falcons!"

He handed me the binoculars. The falcon had dark

patches around its eyes and black-and-white speckled markings. Watching it swoop and soar made something in me feel less cramped and tight. Following it, I caught Mrs. Ingle in my focus. Her arms were outstretched, and, I thought, maybe because Mom had suggested it, she did look sad.

"Let's go back down," I said.

"Grand view, isn't it, dollings?" asked Rosie as we stepped back into her elevator.

"It sure is," said Tony and Mom, but I didn't say anything.

The elevator stopped and in waltzed Marisa Fielding, the most horrible of the horrible girls in the seventh grade class at my new school.

She took one look at me and said, "Oh, *you*! You're that new farmer girl. What are *you* doing here?"

"We're just—" I stammered.

"*I'm* here because I take a master ballet class with Madame Petrovna," said Marisa, her turned-up nose turned up even more than usual. Her hair was scraped back into a tight little bun at the back.

"Are you and Aiden classmates?" Mom asked Marisa, trying to be friendly.

"You could call it that," said Marisa. "I'm frankly just trying to get through this year. I'm applying to a ballet school in Paris, and if I get accepted, believe me, that's where I'm going."

The elevator reached the lobby, and Marisa marched out without saying good-bye.

Four little girls in ballet tutus were waiting for the elevator.

"Dollings!" Rosie held out her arms.

"Gammy!" The little girls rushed into her arms.

"My great-grandbaby ballerinas on their way to their lesson!" Rosie cooed.

"My," said Mom as we walked away, "that Marisa is quite a character!"

I sighed. Mom didn't know half of it.

It was Friday, the end of my third week at the East Park Day School. The day was almost over. I raised my hand to go to the bathroom so I could get out of that classroom for ten minutes.

"Go ahead, Farmer Girl," said Mr. Jenkins. When Mr. Jenkins first heard my name, he said he'd never heard of a girl named Aiden before. Then, when he found out I had lived on a dairy farm and that my last name was Farmer, he started calling me "Farmer Girl." That was typical of his sense of humor.

I went into one of the bathroom stalls and sat there for awhile. I'd never set foot inside a private school before, and every now and then I needed a time-out. The reason I was even going to this school was because Mom had been able to get a job teaching music in the Lower School and I could go for free.

"Amazing educational opportunity, Aiden," both Mom and Tony had said.

Well, maybe, but so far it was only amazingly terrible. For one thing, I had to wear a uniform, a blue plaid skirt, a white blouse, and a blue blazer, and, for another, all the kids were so cityish and cool. And worst of all, I was the *only* new kid in the seventh grade.

I heard giggling now as the door to the bathroom opened.

"Can you believe the stuff that comes out of Adam's mouth? He's been a nerd since the day before he was born. But everyone in this school is just too dull for words."

That was Marisa.

"Do you think *I'm* dull?" I recognized Asha, the girl who was always hanging around Marisa.

"Oh, you're all right," said Marisa in a bored tone of voice. "But you know what? My dance teacher, Madame Petrovna—her studio's in the Ingle Building?" Almost everything Marisa said ended in a question mark. "She says she knows about these gold coins that are lost in the Ingle Building somewhere? They're not really worth a whole lot, but she has a friend who needs gold for something? She can't walk around much anymore because she's old and lame, but she says if I help her find them she'll get me into a ballet school in Paris?"

"That sounds soo exciting," said Asha. "Can I help, too?"

"Well, I don't know how Madame Petrovna would feel about that, but, oh my gosh, look, someone's in here." Marisa's voice dropped to a whisper.

There was silence, and then Asha said in a hushed voice, "I think it's that Farmer Girl. She's wearing those clunky boots."

"Think she's wearing the dumb hat, too? I ran into her at the Ingle Building, and she was even wearing it there!"

Did they think I couldn't hear them? Or did they *want* me to hear them?

"Hey, Asha, let's—"

"Yeah!"

There was more giggling and then the sound of the bathroom door opening and then closing. I came out of the stall wondering what they'd been in such a hurry to do. When I tried to open the bathroom door to the hallway, I found out. I rested my forehead against the door for a minute. First they said mean things about me; then they locked me in the bathroom.

I felt sorry for myself for about five minutes, and then I looked around to see if there was some way of escaping. Sure enough, there was a little window high up on one of the walls. I dragged the trash can over and was about to use it as a stepladder when the door opened.

Mr. Jenkins was standing there, holding a set of keys.

"So sorry about that, Farmer Girl," he said. "I saw the smug way those girls came back to the classroom and, when you didn't return, I figured out what happened. You're not the first who's had that trick played on them, believe me! But don't worry, there will be *consequences*."

"It's okay, Mr. Jenkins," I said. "It's not a big deal." I didn't want kids getting into trouble on my account.

Another older man was standing beside Mr. Jenkins. He was wearing a blue work shirt, the kind that Pops had always worn. He had white hair and shaggy, white eyebrows and a nice, crinkly face. He winked as if to show me he was on my side. I couldn't help smiling back. But as I walked into the classroom, everyone was staring at me and smirking. I felt like crawling into a hole.

Mr. Jenkins stood in front of the class. "Ladies and gentlemen, let it be known that for once and for all, we are taking the lock off the bathroom door, and that will be the end of this silly behavior." He glared at the kids, and Marisa, who sat near me, looked as if she had no idea what he was talking about. "And now, as you can see, Mr. Schwartz is here to wind the clock. I know he's a familiar face around here, so let's just let him get on with his work, and we'll get on with ours."

Mr. Schwartz winked again and waved at the kids and went to the back of the classroom where an old grandfather clock stood in the corner. The school had been a private house a long time ago and had actually belonged to James Ingle, the guy who built the Ingle Building. There were lots of house things in it like the clock and paintings on the walls. Sometimes the whole place felt too fancy for a school, but I liked the clock. It reminded me of home because we had a clock almost exactly like it in our living room, only ours was prettier.

While Mr. Schwartz opened up the glass door that covered the dial, Mr. Jenkins took off his blazer and carefully hung it on the back of his chair. I'd never had a teacher who looked so . . . *ironed*. His straight, black hair was perfectly combed, and his wire-rimmed glasses sat neatly on the end of his nose. "Okay, ladies and gentlemen," he said, "it's time for current events. There is an interesting item in the news today about Gold Falcons."

Marisa's desk was near mine, and I could see her suddenly sit up straight. I have to admit, I sat up straighter, too.

"Remember, ladies and gentlemen," Mr. Jenkins went on, "we have been studying the gold rush of California when all sorts of gold coins were minted. Gold Falcons were among the most beautiful coins ever made in this country." He held up a photograph from the newspaper for us to see. "See, here's one—regard the bird with outspread wings engraved on one side and the lovely head of Liberty on the other. Back then, my friends, these coins were worth five dollars each." He let that sink in, and then he went on, "Ever heard of something called the Depression?"

Adam waved his hand furiously in the air.

"Of course you have, Adam," said Mr. Jenkins without calling on him. "Well, it was hard times for people at the end of the 1920s—people were losing money, banks were failing, the stock market was in trouble, and people who had any gold at all began to hoard it because they thought gold was a safer bet than paper money. They believed its value wouldn't change no matter what was going on."

"What does *hoard* mean?" Marisa asked.

"It means you don't spend it. You keep it to yourself," said Adam. "It's the sort of thing *you* would do."

The look Marisa gave Adam made me shudder, but Adam just grinned at her.

"Yes, that's right, Adam," said Mr. Jenkins. "Well, a law was made that you could no longer use the gold coins to buy things. You were supposed to turn any gold you had back to the U.S. Treasury where it was melted down into gold bars. You weren't even supposed to have gold in your possession, although an exception was made for people who collected rare coins as long as they were not worth more than one hundred dollars."

"That would be twenty Gold Falcons," said Adam.

Mr. Jenkins slapped his knee. "Right you are, my friend, Twenty Gold Falcons! But now, boys and girls, ladies and gentlemen, as of today, Gold Falcons are legal again and—" he paused, "they're worth—well, let's just say they're worth a small fortune."

He was quiet a moment as he waited for this to sink in. Now every pair of eyes was on Mr. Jenkins. Even Mr. Schwartz stopped what he was doing and turned around to stare at him.

"Marisa says—" Asha started to say.

"*Shh*," said Marisa, glaring at Asha. "Don't you dare say *any*thing."

"So, friends, Romans, and countrymen, here's the challenge question of the day," said Mr. Jenkins. "What would you do if you found a collection of Gold Falcons? How would you spend that money?"

"I'd buy a football team," said Chad.

"An entertainment center," said Quentin.

"You already have one," said Adam.

"A better one," said Quentin.

I could feel my stomach begin to churn. I didn't want Mr. Jenkins to call on me.

"I'd put a bowling alley in my house," said Zeke.

"I'd put an Olympic-sized swimming pool in my house," said Brittany.

"What about you, Marisa?" asked Mr. Jenkins.

"I'm—I'm not at liberty to say," said Marisa haughtily.

"But Marisa," Asha said.

Marisa turned and gave her the *Look*.

"*I'd* use it to pay for my Harvard education," said Adam. Everyone turned on him and said, "Boooo."

"Shush," said Mr. Jenkins. "He has a right to his own opinion. And what about you, Farmer Girl?"

I took a deep breath. "I'd keep my farm," I said. "Spiff it up. Fix the roof of the barn." *Shut up, shut up*, I said to myself. *These kids don't care.* But the words kept coming anyway. "Buy a new tractor. Buy more cows."

"That's a good one," said Mr. Jenkins, and I couldn't tell if he meant that's a good one, that's wonderful or that's a good one, what a joke, ha ha, and then someone, I think it was Chad, said, "Moooo," and everyone else started mooing and laughing.

I put my head down on my desk and closed my eyes.

It was dead quiet in the classroom. I wished I had just laughed along with the kids, pretended it was all just a big joke, but now I was paralyzed.

I heard Mr Jenkins clear his throat and say, "They weren't laughing *at* you, Farmer Girl, they were laughing at the mooing." I heard a bit of nervous giggling. "Knock it off, you kids," Mr. Jenkins snapped. "It's the end of the school day, anyway, time for sports. Go on, get out of here."

I heard the sound of chairs being pushed back and all the scuffle and scrambling of packing up. I felt a hand on my shoulder. "Aiden," said Mr. Jenkins.

Wow. What it took for him to call me by my real name. "I'm okay," I mumbled, wanting to get rid of him.

"Well, I hope so," he said. "I have to get to sports. I'll send Mrs. Goodwin up to check on you if you're not out of here in five minutes."

More scuffle and shuffle. Footsteps. And, finally, quiet. Maybe it would be safe for me to sit up and open my eyes now. But no. That old clock guy was sitting at the desk next to mine.

"Not such a great day," he said. "Getting locked in a

bathroom. Having a bunch of kids mooing at you. Having your teacher call you Farmer Girl. What is your real name again?"

"Aiden," I said. "Aiden Farmer." I rubbed my eyes. "I should have laughed it off." Even though I had just met him, Mr. Schwartz was easy to talk to. "Then it would have been funny instead of pathetic."

"Well," said Mr. Schwartz, "it *was* pathetic, the way those kids were going to buy all those things if they came across the Gold Falcons. Yours was the only choice worth thinking about. Hate to think of you losing your farm."

"We haven't actually sold it yet," I said.

Mr. Schwartz got up from the desk and sat on top of it. "If you don't mind me asking you this, Miss Farmer, why *are* you selling it?"

"You could just call me Aiden."

"And you can call me Leo." Leo smiled that crinkly smile of his.

I took a breath. "See, my mom met my dad one summer when she went to work on a dairy farm upstate. He was the dairy farmer, and she fell in love with him. She stayed on the farm and settled down and had me. But then—Pops died—" This was the part I could hardly ever say out loud, but Leo looked so sympathetic everything came out in a rush. "After that, Mom wanted to come back here to live 'cause she still has family here. And also because she wants to pick up the singing career she had before she got married. So that's basically it."

"You don't seem very happy about it," said Leo.

I let out a huge sigh. "I'm not a city kind of person like Mom. She has music in her blood, but I have cows in mine. Moo," I said flatly.

Leo laughed as he got off the desk and headed over to the grandfather clock.

"We have a grandfather clock at home," I said. "It's prettier than this one. It has a picture of a falcon on the face of it. It used to be my job to wind it every eight days."

"Same as this one," said Leo.

I reached my hand into my blazer pocket. "Do you work on other kinds of clocks? Besides grandfather ones?"

"I always say, if it doesn't tick, come tock to me!" said Leo with a laugh. "Yes—all kinds of clocks and watches."

I brought out the old pocket watch Pops had found in the attic along with the hat. Like the hat, he wore it all the time, so now I did, too. As I held it up by the gold chain, Leo's eyes widened.

"It's a beaut," he said, taking it from me. "This is valuable. Real gold. Fine engraving of a bird on the lid. It actually looks a lot like one of those coins your teacher was talking about." He traced a finger around the words engraved in a circle on the back. "*The bird of time flies near,*" he read. He held the watch up to the light, studying it. "Where did you get this?"

I cringed a little. Mom didn't know I had the watch. She had looked everywhere for it and then gave up, thinking it had just gotten lost.

"Pops found it a long time ago in the attic in an old trunk. It doesn't work anymore, though. I can't even open it—the spring is broken or something."

"I'd very much like to take it to my shop and look it over," said Leo. "I can clean it up and fix it for you. I won't charge you."

"Yes, please," I said.

Mrs. Goodwin, the school secretary, suddenly burst into

the room. "Aiden!" she exclaimed. "You *are* still here. Mr. Jenkins told me to come and check on you—you'd better get yourself off to sports."

I started scrambling for my stuff. "Oh my gosh, it's four o'clock, and I am going to be so late!"

"Green Street," he called after me as I raced out of the room. "My shop's number 60 Green Street. Leo's Clock and Watch Shop. Come by tomorrow and pick up your watch."

4

$\mathcal{S}$occer practice was terrible.

Even though I'd played well enough during tryouts to make the JV team, for some reason I was just getting worse and worse. I fumbled and tripped and sometimes even ran in the wrong direction. The coach was frustrated with me, and the girls were flat-out disgusted.

As I walked home through Gill Park, I took the old hat out of my backpack. The minute I put it on, I felt better, a little bit like my old self again anyway.

"Hey! That's a bee-yoo-ti-ful hat, lassie! Bee-yoo-ti-ful."

I nearly jumped out of my skin. Sitting just a few feet away from me on a bench was an old lady screeching at me. She had on a million layers of clothes and almost as many wrinkles on her face. "Hey! I like that hat, lassie! That's bee-yoo-ti-ful! Ha!"

I was so busy staring at her, I didn't see Marisa and Quentin until they were practically in my face.

"There it is!" Quentin yelled.

"Oooh, I want it! Grab it!" Marisa yelled.

Quentin swooped like a vulture, tore the hat off my

head, stuck it on his head, and the two of them stood there laughing like maniacs.

I reached out to grab the hat back, but Quentin and Marisa sped away from me.

"Go on, go after them, they're getting away, go on!" the lady screeched, pointing at their disappearing backs.

I took off, but by the time I caught up, they were sprinting through the gates out of the park, dodging cars as they crossed the big, busy street that ran by the park. I was too scared to dart into the traffic, but then I saw them running up the steps of the East Park Day School.

I finally saw my chance, dashed across, galloped up the front steps, and burst through the door of the school. Mrs. Goodwin was still sitting at her usual place at the front desk.

"Did you see two kids run in just now?" I asked her.

"Oh sure," she said. "Marisa and Quentin. They're in HAH."

"HAH," I echoed, leaning against a wall trying to catch my breath.

"High Achievers' House," she said.

I nodded. Mom had told me about High Achievers', an after-school class where kids could go to get prepped for standardized tests. As soon as Mom had learned about it, she'd told me she thought I should sign up because I was probably academically behind my classmates. No way, I had told her. I didn't want to be in the East Park Day School one minute longer than I had to.

"Where does it meet?" I asked.

"It's down the hall. Room 104," she said, pointing.

I found Room 104 and yanked open the door. The room was filled with kids sitting at desks in rows, papers piled up in front of them. I recognized some of the kids from my homeroom—there was Marisa's friend, Asha, and a prissy girl named Brittany, and know-it-all Adam, and, looking oh-so-innocent, Marisa and Quentin.

"Excuse me, Farmer Girl, may I help you?" I whipped around and saw Mr. Jenkins sitting on a stool at the head of the classroom. "Did you sign up for HAH?"

I gulped. I hadn't even noticed him when I burst into the room.

"Have you signed up?" he repeated.

"Um no," I said. All the kids were staring at me now. "I'm sorry, I am just looking for something." I spotted the hat sitting on top of Quentin's desk. I stalked down the aisle and, as he saw me coming, Quentin's fingers curled around it. I heard the lining rip as I yanked it out of his grasp. I grabbed a piece of paper it was sitting on by accident.

"Thanks," I said.

I was about to toss the piece of paper back at him, but I stood, frozen for a moment. In Marisa's handwriting—I'd seen her big, fat, loopy letters a million times because I sat near her—I read, "Hey, Q, help me go look for the G.Fs. Madame P. says she can give me a clue tomorrow night. Asha wants to, but I don't want her to. She blabs too much." I scrunched the note up into a ball and tossed it at him.

"Well, if you change your mind, Farmer Girl," Mr. Jenkins said as I was leaving.

I stood outside in the hallway for a moment, holding the hat, looking at the torn lining. I felt terrible, like something inside me had been torn. Why did Quentin have to do that? I jammed it back onto my head.

"No hats in the school building, dear," said Mrs. Goodwin as I passed by her desk.

"For Pete's sake!" I yelled.

I went back into the park. The light was fading, and the street lamps had been turned on. Tony had told me about an apartment overlooking the park where musicians signed up to play—almost always there was something—trumpet, or piano, or violins, coming into the park through speakers. Right now someone was playing the harmonica.

I was sort of bouncing along to the harmonica music, feeling better, when I became aware that the ripped lining inside the hat made it feel lumpy. I took it off. Peeking out from underneath the lining was a small square of white cloth sewn into the cap. I pulled back the lining a little more. There was writing on the square in tiny, black, capital letters: FLY TO E15.

I stared and stared at it.

What was *that* doing in my hat? Then, slowly, the wheels began turning in my head. The hat, after all, wasn't mine. Pops had worn it, but he had found it in a trunk in the attic. Our attic was like a regular junk shop. There was a ton of stuff in it from Dad's family, and every time relatives on Mom's side of the family moved we got all their things. So who had the hat belonged to? A Farmer or a Balboni?

I had been walking the whole time I was thinking, and I found myself standing in front of the park fountain. At night it was lit up by colored lights that changed every few seconds. A beautiful red, feathery spray of water leaped up now . . . and then it turned green . . . then yellow . . . and then blue. It was like watching fireworks. I stood staring in a trance, forgetting everything for a moment, and then suddenly the entire area around the fountain filled up with black figures, all laughing and jumping and yelling. It dawned on me that I was watching a bunch of kids dressed up in hairy black gorilla suits. Some were wearing gorilla masks, some not, but they were all either carrying baseball gloves or bats or both.

"Tough game!" one of them said.

"Yeah! Really tough!" said another.

"Did you see the look on that dumb pitcher's face when I whaled it out to left field?" a tall gorilla asked a short gorilla. "He couldn't believe I could hit like that." The tall gorilla whipped off its mask, and I was stunned to see Marisa.

I stormed over to her. "Hey! Why'd you lock me in the bathroom? And why'd you steal my hat?" I never would have spoken to her like that at school but being out in the park made me feel brave.

Marisa stared at me, frowning, as if she didn't have the slightest idea what I was talking about. Someone grabbed her by her hairy arm, and the whole group moved on. I didn't have the nerve to go after her, and it didn't occur to me until I was climbing the stairs to Tony's apartment to wonder how Marisa could have been there in a gorilla suit when I'd just seen her at HAH.

I was still thinking about Marisa as I fumbled around with the keys, unlocking the zillion locks on Tony's door. It was so annoying. We never locked our farmhouse at home.

Henrietta, my cat, came right over and rubbed against my leg. I had wanted to bring Nellie and Hector, our dogs, with us to Gloria, but Mom said city life would be too hard on them. Uncle Tony was the one who said I could bring Henrietta. Nellie and Hector had gone to live with Blake.

Mom was sitting on the couch, the fold-out that doubled as her bed. She looked up from her laptop computer as I came in. "I wish you would call me if you're going to be late," she said.

"Something came up," I said.

"Okay, but I worry, you know." She went back to staring at her computer.

Tony had done his best to rearrange his apartment when we moved in, but as I looked around, I hated how cramped and crowded everything was. I didn't even know where to put down my stuff. Mom slept in the living room, where the piano used to be. I slept in a bed Tony had made for me—a wooden frame with sides high enough so I wouldn't fall out, bolted into the ceiling and hanging just high enough so Tony didn't bonk his head every time he walked around. I had to climb up on a bookcase to get onto it. Once I was in, there wasn't a lot of room between me and the ceiling, but it was the one place I could go and feel as if I had a little privacy.

I knew I should be grateful Mom and I even had a place to stay. The farmhouse hadn't sold yet, and Mom had only just started working. Tony said we were helping him out by living with him because an opera singer has to travel a lot and he liked the idea of us being in the apartment to keep an eye on things. Mom and I both knew he was just being nice to us. The good thing for him, at least, was that he was able to keep his own bedroom.

Mom looked up from the computer. "Well, how was your day?" she asked in a fake, bright tone.

"My day was *fine*," I said. I knew she would not want to hear about me being locked in the bathroom or having my hat stolen by stupid kids. She looked frazzled. She also didn't look like herself. Ever since we'd moved from the country, she'd started wearing different clothes. Instead of old sweaters and jeans, she was wearing artsy tops and necklaces and pleated skirts and tights. Instead of sneakers, she was wearing high heels. "How was your day?" I asked.

"I'm never going to break into the coffeehouse scene here," she said with a sigh. "I'm too old. I've missed my chance."

I had to bite my tongue not to say something mean. "Mom, have you heard about the Gold Falcons? They're worth a lot now."

Keeping her eyes on the computer, Mom said vaguely, "That's nice. Well, maybe you *should* go and try to find them."

I tried a different topic. "Who do you think Pops's old hat belonged to?" This time she looked up.

"Oh, I suppose it could have been Grandpa Balboni," she said. "I certainly remember him wearing a hat like that. But maybe Grandpa Farmer did, too. Never met him, but I seem to remember seeing photos of him in that kind of hat."

I was about to show her the little note inside the hat, but she was back to staring at her computer. I went into the little room that was Tony's office. It had a desk and a computer and stacks of sheet music, and it was also where Tony's piano now lived. I checked my e-mail, and there was a message from Blake, which was a miracle because he hated writing.

"Hey, Aiden. Thought you'd like to know—Alfalfa and all the other girls are with us now. Pops bought them all at auction. The guy who bought them before couldn't keep them. Nellie and Hector are doing great."

Well, that was good news. The "girls," our cows, were now living just down the road from where they'd lived most of their lives. I was glad Nellie and Hector were doing well, too, although thinking about them made me sad again.

I clicked into a folder where we had photos of the farm. There was Blake on a payloader, holding up a blue ribbon he'd won for the calf he'd raised. I'd forgotten how big and muscley he was, not scrawny and wimpy-looking like Quentin.

And there was a picture of me hugging Clover, my favorite cow. Back then I had rosy cheeks and my hair was down to my waist. Now I was pale and hardly had any hair. The day Mom told me we were going to sell the farm, I'd gone and chopped it all off.

I clicked out of the folder and sat with the hat in my lap. FLY TO E15. I really wished I knew what it meant.

The next morning I decided to get up and take Henrietta to the park. Poor cat, all cooped up in an apartment when she was used to having the whole world as her hunting territory.

Peering over the edge of my bed, I saw that Mom was up, too, lesson plan books piled around her on the couch even though it was Saturday morning.

I slid off my bed, stepped onto the bookcase, and climbed down to the floor. I went into the bathroom and threw on a T-shirt and jeans, came out, grabbed a jacket and my hat and the long, thin piece of rope I'd bought to use as a leash for Henrietta.

"Don't forget, we're going to Mitch's this afternoon to meet his adopted daughter."

"Yeah, yeah," I said, feeling lousy at the thought of having to meet another city kid. She wouldn't like me, and I wouldn't like her.

"And we have Tony's opera tonight."

I made a face, and Mom sighed as I slipped a collar around Henrietta's neck and tied the rope to it. Scooping her up into my arms, I was out the door. I managed to cross the street and get into the park before she clawed me to death. When I finally let her leap to the ground, she just stood there, the breeze riffling her tiger-striped fur. It was as if she didn't know what to do outdoors anymore.

I looked around. I had the whole park to myself except for a few joggers. No one was playing music, but the crows were having a party up in the top of an oak tree. The leaves were beginning to turn, and I could feel the cold air on my face.

Henrietta took a step and instantly got tangled up in the rope. As I was crouching down trying to help her, I heard footsteps, but I didn't catch on to what was happening until too late. "Gotcha!" I heard someone yell and felt a hand on my hat. Just in time, I clutched at it, and then I saw Quentin standing there with a crazy look in his eyes. He pulled and I pulled. The lining ripped even more.

"GET OUTTA HERE, YOU STINKING BRAT!" A scrawny girl in overalls appeared out of nowhere, yelling her head off. She was holding a baseball glove and shaking it at him. Quentin stood with his mouth hanging open, staring at the girl in disbelief as he let go of the hat.

"I said get outta here," the girl said fiercely. She stood with her hands on her hips and glared at Quentin. "Or I'll spit on you." She took a step toward Quentin, making a disgusting sound in her throat. I sat back on my heels and laughed at the expression on his face. He looked as if he might throw up. "You can have your dumb old hat," he said. "I never wanted it anyway. It was all Marisa's idea." He turned on his heels and walked away.

"Thanks," I said to the girl.

"No problem," she said. "But I gotta zip outta here. Places to go, people to meet."

I watched her disappearing back, wishing I had had more

of a chance to find out who she was. Then I slapped the hat back on my head, thinking I might as well head back to the apartment. But just as I was about to gather up Henrietta, a black cat poked its head out from behind a tree. Henrietta's ears instantly went back, her fur puffed up, and she started hissing. The black cat approached her anyway and put out a friendly paw. Henrietta slowly backed away, still hissing and spitting.

"I don't think this cat is out to get you, Henrietta," I said.

The black cat came up to me and rubbed against my legs. I crouched down to pet it. A cute little mew came out of its pink mouth and then with its tail straight up in the air, it walked a few feet away from us and then stopped, turning slightly, and mewed again.

"Hey, Henrietta, it wants us to follow."

I picked up Henrietta, rope and all, and began to follow the cat. The park was filling up with more people now, and a man with a chocolate lab on a leash walked by. The lab approached the cat, and the two of them rubbed noses, the dog's tail wagging like crazy.

"Hello Jack," the man said to the cat, stooping down to pet him.

Jack trotted ahead of us, stopping to watch a woman who was feeding crumbs to a flock of pigeons. He didn't chase them, and the pigeons didn't seem at all disturbed by the cat.

Next stop was the old woman who'd liked my hat yesterday. She was back sitting on her bench, still dressed in all her layers. "Ha! Black Jack!" she screeched, bending over to pet the cat. Then she saw me. "Hat Girl! And now you have a cat! A hat and a cat!" she cackled.

We came to a gate that led out of the park. And straight

ahead of me across the street was a store with a large sign saying LEO'S CLOCK AND WATCH REPAIR SHOP. IF IT DOESN'T TICK, COME TOCK TO US.

"Oh! Black Jack!" I exclaimed. "How did you know? I almost forgot!"

Black Jack rubbed against my leg and then turned and ran back into the park.

I crossed the street. As I went in the door of the shop, I hoped Leo wouldn't mind me bringing Henrietta in with me. He was sitting up at a high counter. He had a magnifying eyeglass in one eye and a tiny little screwdriver in one hand, and springs and screws were spread out in front of him. The eyeglass dropped out of his eye when he saw me. "Ah Aiden, wonderful! And you've brought a friend with you. Don't worry—cats are welcome!"

I looked around. There were so many clocks, of all sizes and shapes, hanging up on the walls, sitting on shelves and tables, standing on the floor. A glass case was filled with watches with all sorts of watchbands.

As I put Henrietta down, Leo reached under the counter and pulled up a box. Opening it, he carefully took out the pocket watch. It was all cleaned up, the gold gleaming and beautiful, the engraving of the bird standing out clearly.

"I took the lid off by unscrewing the hinge here," he said, pointing with the screwdriver. "My, but it was gummed up with dirty oil and who knows what else. What is the story of this watch, Aiden? Where exactly did it come from?" He was looking at me intently.

"My dad wore this hat," I said, pointing to it, "and the watch all the time. He liked old-fashioned things. So when he died, I—"

"You wore them to keep him with you," said Leo gently. "But now, let's see if I understand this. The watch comes from your father's side of the family?"

"I'm not sure. It could be Farmer or Balboni, it's hard to know."

Leo's eyes widened. *"Balboni?* Any relation to the musical Balbonis?"

"Yes, Fortunato Balboni was my great-grandpa—you've heard of him?"

Leo struck a hand to his forehead. "Heard of him! I *knew* him! Lovely old gentleman. Very kind to my parents. He was the one who got them jobs as elevator operators at the Ingle Building when they first landed in this country."

"Rosie!" I exclaimed. "I know her!"

"That's my old ma," Leo said. "And my old pa, Ernie, works Mrs. Ingle's elevator."

A cuckoo sprang out of its house and cuckooed, and all sorts of clocks bonged as if they were as happy to find this out as I was.

"It's a small world, isn't it?" said Leo. "I knew your grandparents before they moved to Florida—they played in the Gloria Symphony Orchestra at the Ingle Building, as I'm sure you know—and Antonio Balboni must be your uncle, and your mother is Allegra—"

"She's the music teacher at my school now," I said. "I'm surprised you haven't run into her."

"Now that you mention it, I *have* seen her there. I thought she looked familiar. And once again, Aiden, I'm so sorry about your father."

We were both quiet for a moment, and then, tracing a finger lightly over the engraving of the bird on the watch, Leo said, "The Balboni connection explains a lot. This is a falcon, which is the symbol of the Ingle family. When I first saw it yesterday, I did wonder. But it's the inside that tells the real story." He pressed the knob on top of the watch lightly with his thumb. The lid sprang open. "Now take a look at this."

There were two sets of initials engraved in fancy script on the inside cover of the lid. "From F.B. to E.I.," I read aloud.

"Fortunato Balboni to Edward Ingle," said Leo. "A gift from one to the other. Fortunato was great friends with Edward Ingle."

I scratched my head. "But, *from* F.B. to E.I. I don't understand. If my great-grandpa gave it to Edward Ingle, why would *we* have it?"

"It must have come back to your Balboni relatives for some reason—perhaps after Edward Ingle died. In any case, it still runs like a charm." He handed it to me. "If you're going to carry it around with you, though, you must be careful. It's quite valuable."

I held it in my hand, afraid to slip it back into my pocket the way I always had before. Leo came out from behind the counter. "Here, pin the chain to your shirt. That way you can't lose it."

He helped me with the pin and then, taking the hat off, I turned it upside down and pulled back the lining. "Leo," I said, "look what I found in the hat."

"FLY TO E15," he read slowly. Then he said, "Aiden Farmer!" His eyes were bright. "Do you know what you have here? My sister and I used to play with the Ingle children when we were growing up. Before Mr. Ingle died, he and your great-granddad loved nothing better than to set up clues for us and make us run all over the Ingle Building after some kind of treasure. The last hunt they ever set up was for the Gold Falcons."

My heart started racing. "Rosie was telling us about it. How they were never found."

"Well, Aiden, it was a long time ago, and I was pretty young, but seeing this is stirring something in my old brain. I'm remembering the kind of clues we would get. Some of 'em were just like this. FLY TO E15. And that would mean we were supposed to go to the east wing on the 15th floor." He threw the hat up in the air, laughing out loud with delight. "Fly to E15, my friend, and find those Falcons and save your farmhouse."

My legs were trembling and, to make things worse, Henrietta had managed to wind herself completely around my ankles. I bent down and unwound her. As I straightened up, I said, "This girl in my class, Marisa Fielding, has a dance teacher, Madame Petrovna, who says she remembers the treasure hunt and is going to give Marisa a clue."

Leo laughed. "Natasha! Nan Peters she was in those days. I can still picture her racing down those hallways, wanting to be the first to find those clues! She changed her name and put on an accent when she became a ballet dancer. She became very good, mind you, but to me she'll always be little Nan." He handed me back the hat. "But if she and Marisa are after the gold, all the more reason for you to get going, Aiden."

I was just gathering up Henrietta when Leo said, "You know, I remember now that Mr. Ingle told a story that was part of the treasure hunt. It was about a girl who went looking for gold, and she had to get past trolls. You had to listen carefully because there were clues in it. . . . Of course, I can't at all remember what the clues were."

The door opened, and a man and a woman came into the store.

"How much do I owe you for the watch, Leo?" I asked.

"No, no, I told you, no charge," he said. "The prospect of hunting for Gold Falcons again, that is payment enough. Just keep me up to date on what you find, and I'll keep trying to remember that story."

Skipping out of Leo's shop, I heard someone shouting my name. "Hey, Aiden! Aiden!" I turned around to see who could be calling me. It was Adam, and he was dragging along one of those rolling backpacks. I put my hat back on and said, "Hi, Adam," as calmly as I could.

Adam's hair was tufted up, as if he'd been pulling on it, which I know he did all the time because I sat near him in the classroom. He was wearing a very ironed, blue, button-down shirt tucked into khaki pants. His sneakers looked so white they made you want to step on them and get them dirty.

"Did you sign up for High Achievers?" he asked.

"No," I said, "why would I?"

"Well, so you can get high scores on tests."

I made a face at him. "I bet you already do well on all kinds of tests."

"Yeah, well," he said with a shrug, "my parents put a lot of pressure on me. So what were you doing there yesterday if you weren't signing up?"

"I was trying to get my hat back," I said. Adam looked puzzled. "Marisa and Quentin stole my hat."

"That seems pointless," he said.

"Yeah, well."

He bit his lip slightly, looking embarrassed. "I didn't moo at you, by the way."

I turned hot at the memory.

"Well, I'm running a little late and you get points taken off if you're late, so I'd better go," he said.

"Where are you going?" I asked.

"To HAH, of course," he said, as if that were obvious.

I frowned at him. "But it's Saturday."

"Yeah, it is," he said.

I couldn't quite believe it. "This is what you *do* on Saturday? You go to a class so you can get higher test scores when your test scores are probably already as high as they can get?"

"Oh no, they could be higher. I need to get perfect scores." He didn't even crack a smile. "See you later, Aiden."

"Wait a minute, wait a minute, Adam."

A million things were racketing through my brain. "There are Gold Falcons hidden somewhere in the Ingle Building," I blurted out. "And I found a clue to where they are in my hat."

"Okay, that's nice," he said, "but I have to go." As he started to leave, I ran after him.

"Look, I'll show you." I swiped the hat off my head and shoved it under his nose. "Read what it says on that little piece of cloth inside the lining."

"FLY TO E15," Adam read.

"It's a clue. It means go to the east wing, 15th floor."

Adam frowned. "I'm confused. Why would some weird writing in your hat have anything to do with Gold Falcons in the Ingle Building?"

"My great-grandfather was the impresario at the Ingle

Building," I said. I liked the word *impresario*. It seemed so *impressive*. Adam was looking at me blankly. Smart as he was, he didn't know what an impresario was. "That's a word for a person who's in charge of musical performances—and that's what my great-grandfather, Fortunato Balboni, did at the Ingle Building. This hat came out of a trunk in our attic. I think it belonged to my great-grandfather who was very good friends with Edward Ingle. The two of them hid the Gold Falcons for a treasure hunt."

Adam finally stopped walking and stood still and listened to me.

"I just came from Leo's shop—he's the guy who comes to our school to wind the clock, you know, and he just told me Mr. Ingle left clues just like this one." I waved the hat in his face. "So now, do you get it?" I said. "If I find the Gold Falcons, I can keep the farm. I can buy more cows. You can go to Harvard."

Why, I wondered, half angry with myself, was I choosing Adam to share all this with. Then I had to admit that if Marisa had Quentin to help her, I wanted someone helping me. It wouldn't hurt that he was obviously the smartest kid in our class.

"I say we go look for the Falcons right now, and if we find them we'll share them," I said.

"What? *Now?* I have to go to HAH right now."

"You could skip it."

"I can't skip it," he said. "If I skip it, I won't get *into* Harvard."

"Well, later, this afternoon," I said, remembering I was supposed to meet Mom at the tree house.

"I have to do homework this afternoon and practice the piano."

"You can't do homework and practice all day," I said, exasperated. "Listen, Adam. I happen to know Marisa Fielding and Quentin Bolter are going after those coins."

Adam's eyes sort of fluttered, and I could tell I had finally reached him. "Let me see the hat again."

I took off the hat, and Adam took it from me and stared at it while I stared at the goofy gap between his two front teeth. "I can meet you tomorrow. Late morning," he said. "You're going to need help if you're going to find those things before Marisa and Quentin." We exchanged phone numbers, and then he rushed away, his backpack rumbling and tipping from side to side because he was running so fast.

I crossed into the park, thinking how I'd always been the kind of girl who hung out more with boys than with girls, but Adam wasn't like any boy I'd ever hung out with before. I went over to a tree and tied up Henrietta. Someone was playing a Beatles tune on the piano into the park. I stood leaning against the tree, listening to the song. If I closed my eyes, I could imagine I was home, sitting at the table in the big, old kitchen, doing my homework, with Mom playing the piano in the next room.

If I found the Gold Falcons, Mom and I could go back home.

Then I remembered I was supposed to meet Mom at Mitch's tree house. I'd take Henrietta back to the apartment and then go over. But when I looked down, the leash and the collar were on the ground, and Henrietta was nowhere to be seen.

Mitch Bloom's tree house was up in a huge oak tree. Mom and I stood beneath it. I was wailing. "Mom, Henrietta got away!"

Mom put a hand on my shoulder. "Oh, Aiden," was all she said.

"What am I going to do?" The tears were streaming down my face.

Mom bit her lip. "She's a smart cat, she'll be okay."

"But she won't know how to get back to Tony's. And she doesn't know about cars."

Mom closed her eyes for a moment. Then she opened them and said, "We'll ask Mitch to keep an eye out for her. If anyone can find her, he can."

She patted me comfortingly and then opened a gray, metal box mounted on the trunk of Mitch's oak tree and pressed a button that made a buzzing sound.

"Howdy!" A scratchy voice came through a speaker that was also mounted on the trunk.

"It's Allegra and Aiden," Mom said, putting her mouth close to the speaker. It looked funny, as if she were talking to the tree.

"Wonderful!" said the voice. "I've been expecting you. Come on up."

A plywood box came rumbling and rattling down on steel rods from the tree house. We climbed in, and when the elevator stopped at the top and Mom opened the door there was cousin Mitch just as I remembered him, a tall, skinny man with a whole lot of springy, curly hair and a big, bobbing Adam's apple.

"Greetings, greetings," said Mitch. He pulled me out of the elevator and gave me a huge hug. "You've grown like a weed," he said. And then more seriously, "I'm so pleased you came back to Gloria, cousins, but I expect it will take some getting used to." He must have noticed that I had been crying. "Being transplanted is no joke, but you'll grow new roots soon enough." He patted my head. "Nice hat, by the way."

Then Mom and I told him about Henrietta and, after we had described her in detail, Mitch said, "I'm on it. Not to worry. Really, Aiden, I'll find her."

Feeling a little better, I was able to take in the house. I loved it as much now as I had when I'd been younger. There was the tiny living room with a couch, an easy chair, a desk, and paintings on the walls. Through a door, I could see the little kitchen with its miniature woodstove.

"Come, sit," said Mitch. He went into the kitchen and came back out with some glasses of lemonade and a plate of cookies. "Liesl should be home soon. She had a baseball game this afternoon."

"Are you really in charge of Gill Park now, Mitch?" Mom asked.

Mitch nodded. "I work with that boy, Willy Wilson, the one who inherited the park from Otto Pettingill. Willy has done a mighty good job. Kept the developers at bay. Seems like there's always someone who wants this parkland for something." He pulled at his springy hair and his Adam's apple bounced. "But what with the stock market falling so much recently, I'm afraid the money Otto Pettingill set aside for the park seems to be getting smaller and smaller every day. Don't mind telling you," he said with a shake of head, "I'm worried about it. We're trying to figure out ways to raise funds so we can keep everything going without selling off any of the land."

"Oh, everything is about money these days," said Mom, a frown between her eyes.

There was a long buzzing sound followed by a bunch of short buzzes. "That'll be Liesl now," said Mitch. "I'll just send the elevator down."

The whole tree vibrated as the elevator went down and then came back up. The door opened, and a girl wearing a gorilla suit flung herself into the room. "Guess what, guess what, guess what!" she screeched. "Frankie wants me to spend the night!" I was startled to realize she was the girl who had yelled at Quentin.

"Whoa, careful there, Liesl, we've got company," said Mitch. Liesl came to a complete stop, looking me up and down. "I know you," she said. "You're the girl with the hat."

"Yeah," I said. "Thanks for helping me today."

"If there's anything I can't stand, it's a bully," she said. "What's your name again?"

"Aiden," I said.

"Oh yeah, Aiden Farmer," she said. "You're the one who's a cousin." She stepped forward and grabbing my hand, started shaking it. "I'm Liesl Summer. Pleased ta meet ya."

"You, too," I said, wincing slightly as she pumped my arm up and down.

"And this is Aiden's mom—"

"You're my cousin, too, Mitch Bloom told me," she said to Mom. "First cousin once removed, removed from what I don't really know. And also," she said, turning back to me, "you're half an orphan. I'm a whole orphan."

Mom and I stared at her, a little floored by her bluntness.

Mitch put a hand on Liesl's arm. "Go easy now. Try to think before you speak, Liesl. I'm sorry," he said, turning to us with an apologetic look on his face, "this little flower can be a bit wild sometimes. How was the game, Liesl?"

"It really stank," said Liesl, scowling. She began to peel off the gorilla outfit. "Our third baseman called at the last minute to say he couldn't play. Robby Wildman subbed, and he's terrible, and Willy Wilson struck out every time, and I cannot tell a lie—I struck out, too. Thursday's a crucial game, and, if we lose, we lose the postseason match. Come on, Aiden, I'll show you my room."

Her bad mood about losing the baseball game seemed to vanish, and I had to be quick to follow her as she scrambled up a ladder standing at the back of the tree house. We went up through a hatch, out onto a staircase right out in the open air.

Liesl popped through another hatch into a little room. "It's called Liesl's Palace," she said proudly. It was snug with a bed and a chair and a rug. Across one window was a shelf with colored glass bottles on it. The light came through them, filling the room with a blue and yellow and rosy glow.

Liesl sat down on her bed, which had a patchwork quilt on it. She patted the space next to her and said, "Here, you can sit down." As I sat down, she said, "I never had much don't-do-this or don't-do-that stuff when I was little, so that's why I say things I shouldn't sometimes. Mr. Otto Pettingill who used to own Gill Park was my guardian after my parents got killed. I lived in an apartment with a lady who took care of me, but he didn't believe in schools. Somehow he fixed it so I didn't have to go. I hung out in the park all the time and drew pictures with chalk on the pavement. I got real good at it, but it was *awful* not going to school. Then he died, and Mitch Bloom adopted me, and I started going to school a year ago, and I love it, and I am *finally* making friends." She rushed all this out and then took a breath and asked, "Where do you go to school?"

"The East Park Day School," I said, feeling my life was pretty tame compared to hers.

"I feel sorry for you," said Liesl. "My friend, Frankie, has a sister who goes there, and it's a stuck-up kind of place."

"Yeah, it is," I agreed. "Who's her sister? Maybe I know her."

"Marisa Fielding," said Liesl.

"Oooh," I said, my voice giving away how I felt about Marisa.

"Not your favorite person, huh?"

"Well, I don't think she likes *me* very much. I don't know why. I just met her, and I never did anything to her."

"Marisa and Frankie are twins who look exactly like each other," said Liesl.

"Oohh," I said again, understanding now how Marisa had seemed to be in two places at once yesterday. "Frankie must play on your gorilla baseball team."

"Frankie got all the good-at-playing-sports genes and Marisa got all the good-at-ballet ones," said Liesl. "And Frankie says the best thing that ever happened was not having to go to the same school as her. You should quit your school and go to mine. Only a few kids go there, and everyone gets along, and in the afternoons you get to choose what you want to learn. Right now I'm studying sculpture."

"Did—did you mind—about your parents?" I blurted out. Liesl was absolutely still for a moment. I could have kicked myself for saying anything. "I'm sorry," I said. "It's just you mentioned being an orphan, and it doesn't seem like you mind talking about it—and—my dad died just about a year ago."

Liesl reached over and punched me on my arm. I think it was meant to be a friendly punch, but it actually hurt quite a bit. "Hey, that's too bad," she said. "For me it happened a long time ago. I don't really remember my parents, although I dream about them sometimes. You want to know something?" She leaned her face close into mine. Her skin was very fair, and I could see a little blue vein above the bridge of her nose. "Sometimes I dream my mom and dad and I are climbing trees together. Going up through the branches, and the sun is shining on the leaves, and I can hear them rustling—the leaves, not my parents." She was quiet for a minute. "I have this idea that when my parents died, they turned into trees. You know those kind of stories? My old guardian, Mr. Pettingill, would tell stories like that sometimes—about people turning into trees or rivers. Well, there are two trees in the middle of the woods here, and they kind of twine round each other, and I think they are my mom and dad. I go and sit right in the middle of them sometimes."

Then she reached over and grabbed my arm. "You don't think I'm a weirdo, do you? That's what Marisa thinks. She hates it when I come over. Frankie and I have the best time being as weird as we can around her." She started cackling like an old witch, and I couldn't help laughing with her. It made me feel so much better about Marisa.

A voice came out of a speaker on her wall. "Allegra has to go," we heard Mitch say. "And she wants to know if Aiden is staying or going."

"She's staying," said Liesl, reaching out and punching me again. I was beginning to like her, but I wished she wouldn't punch so much. "We'll go tree climbing, you and me, okay? You're my cousin, after all. I've never had a cousin before. We can go right outside my window. You'll like that, right?"

"Of course," I said. "I love climbing trees."

A black cat suddenly popped into the room through a partially open window. "Hey, Black Jack!" said Liesl.

"Black Jack is *your* cat!" I exclaimed. He leaped up onto the bed and then a second later Henrietta came in the window. She jumped up on the bed, too.

"Henrietta!" I pulled her into my lap. "She's my cat, and I thought I lost her!"

"Naw, just hangin' out in the 'hood," said Liesl. "Come on, let's go!" Liesl crawled out her window and Jack, Henrietta, and I followed. We spent all afternoon in the tree.

Henrietta and I were back at Tony's apartment. I was sitting at Tony's computer e-mailing some of my friends
from home. Linda Woolner was filling me in on all the gos-
sip of the seventh grade. It was hard to believe all the stuff
that was going on without me.

Mom stuck her head in the door. "We should be getting
ready to go pretty soon," she said.

I swiveled around in Tony's office chair. "Where are we
going?"

"Tony's opera," she said. "Remember?"

I groaned. I had totally forgotten. "Do I have to go?"

"Yes, of course," she said, getting huffy. "We missed his
opening night because we were packing up the house, and
it's the least we can do. Tony's a bit nervous tonight—some
important people are going to be in the audience."

I swiveled in the chair again. "I hate opera. It is so
screechy and weird."

"*The Marriage of Figaro* isn't," said Mom. "And the
more you go to opera, the more you'll appreciate it. It's
an acquired taste, like learning to like olives. And wear

something nice," she added, backing out of the room. "Tony's girlfriend, Merla, is coming, and she always looks so stunning."

"I'll never like olives, and I don't have anything nice to wear," I said. "And I don't care about Merla, she's—" I stopped, remembering with a jolt about the Gold Falcons. *I could start looking for them.*

"You have that outfit we bought the other day," said Mom, poking her head back in.

"Oh yeah," I said. "The *fantastic* outfit." ("It looks *fantastic*," Mom and the store clerk kept saying.)

"And Aiden, please don't wear that hat," said Mom.

"For Pete's sake!" I yelled, but she had already shut the door. I started planning. Maybe during an intermission I could start looking around. Excited now, I headed for the bathroom. My "closet" consisted of a wobbly rack Tony had set up for me in there. The top and the skirt to the outfit had fallen off the hanger and were bunched on the floor. I put them on and stared in disbelief at myself in the mirror. "Mom," I yelled, "I'm not an 'outfit' kind of person."

I could actually hear her groaning through the closed door.

Mom cooked chicken and potatoes and broccoli. She cleared off the high counter that set off the living room/ Mom's bedroom from the kitchen. Usually it was cluttered with sheets of music and CDs. Since moving, we mostly ordered in Chinese or pizza and sat eating straight out of the boxes on Mom's couch. It was a treat to be sitting up on one of Tony's stools, eating a real meal.

"That was good, Mom," I said when we had finished.

"Thank you, and you look pretty," she said.

"Pretty might be overdoing it," I said. "But you look great." And she did look nice—she had on a fern-green dress and pearls, and her hair, a dark blonde, wasn't short and spiky like mine but long and wavy.

"We'll leave the dishes for later," she said. "We're running a little late, and it's starting to rain so we'll grab a taxi. Tony took the car earlier." Mom had brought our car to Gloria, and Tony, who didn't have a car of his own, often used it. "Here's your raincoat, sweetie."

"I don't need a stupid raincoat—" but Mom was glaring at me, so I put the raincoat on.

We walked down the stairs of Tony's apartment, and Mom, holding an umbrella over her head, stood halfway out in the street so she could hail a taxi. Sometimes I was amazed by how at ease Mom was in the city.

A taxi pulled up, and Mom and I scrambled into it. "Ingle Building, please," said Mom as we got in. I hadn't been in that many taxis in Gloria, but the few I had been in had a Plexiglas divider between the driver and the passengers, and some even had a computer screen. This one just seemed like someone's old car, not a taxi at all, and there was a nice cologne and leather seat smell.

The driver, a big man with a shaved head, swiveled around and grinned at us. One of his front teeth was made of gold. His skin was the color of coffee, and he had a nice accent that I couldn't quite place. "Where are you going tonight?"

"The Ingle Building," said Mom

"Ingle, eh?" His accent made Ingle sound like Een-go-lee. "What brings you there?" he asked, warm and friendly.

"We're going to the opera," said Mom. "And, um, I think we're running a little late—so if you don't mind—"

"I am hearing the opera is very good—the man who sings Figaro, Antonio Balboni, they say he is"—the driver kissed his fingertips—"*fabuloso!*"

"Oh, that's wonderful," Mom said, pleased. "He's—"

There was a screeching of brakes ahead of us, and the driver slammed on his brakes, yelling out, *"Ai! Ai! Bacalhau!"* Mom and I lurched forward. *"Opa!"* he exclaimed. "That was a close call!" He lowered his window and stuck his head out. "Oh, I see now! There's some kind of trouble up there!"

Opening his door, he scrambled out of the cab and strode right through the middle of the traffic in the pouring rain. All the cars around us started honking. Mom and I looked at each other.

"Good grief," said Mom. "I hope this isn't going to make us late."

We sat, and I could feel Mom getting more and more stressed.

"His name is Fernando Costa," I said, leaning forward to read the license on the dashboard. "And that's a Brazilian flag."

Mom sighed. "Well, at least the meter isn't running." More waiting. Mom sighed again. "They speak Portuguese in Brazil," she said after a moment.

"I know—we studied South America in third grade, remember?" I said. "It wasn't like we didn't learn anything just because we were a country school."

"I didn't say that, Aiden."

Before either of us could say anything more, Fernando

Costa returned. He was carrying a large bird, holding it close to his chest. Opening the passenger door in the front with one hand, he said, "Poor bird! I am afraid it could be Lady Peregrine, the one who lives up in the Een-go-lee with the *Senhora*. She will be very upset—she loves those birds!" A strong, wet, animal smell filled the cab. "Too much rain, she doesn't see the wires, and *pppzzt*, she falls into the road. Lucky she doesn't get run over." Fernando took off his jacket and making a sort of nest out if it, placed the bird in it. Leaning forward, I could see her big, frightened eyes. She was making little panting noises and trembling.

"Hey, man, hurry it up!" The guy in the car next to us was yelling out his window.

Fernando came back around to his side of the car and climbed in behind the wheel and started driving again. "Poor Lady," he said again, "sometimes it's not so good when the wild birds come to live in the city."

"Is she badly hurt, do you think?" asked Mom.

"Not so sure," he said. "Maybe it is just the shock, you know?"

The falcon *erked* and stirred a little.

"S'okay, birdie," said Fernando, "I take you to the Bird Lady, to a warm, safe place. She'll fix you up good. But, I better get moving if you are going to make it to your opera."

Fernando seemed to spend more time looking at the falcon than where he was driving. Mom grabbed my arm once when the cab swerved, barely missing a motorcycle. As we finally pulled up in front of the Ingle Building, Mom fished into her purse to pay the fare.

"No charge," Fernando said, putting out a hand to stop her. "Because I keep you waiting."

"Thank you," said Mom, "you are very kind."

"Okay," said Fernando, "you better fly."

"*Fly?*" It made me think of FLY TO E15.

"Aiden," said Mom, pulling me by the arm, "come on. We're going to be late."

Mom and I came out of the dark, rainy night into the almost too bright, huge lobby with plush, cranberry-red carpets with yellow falcons woven into them. Everything seemed to be gleaming, from the huge crystal chandeliers hanging from the ceilings to the giant, polished wood tables. A lot of men and women in cranberry-colored uniforms were standing around with yellow braid on their shoulders and shiny falcons pinned to the brims of their caps.

Mom pulled me past restaurants and gift shops, a barber shop, a health club with a ton of people sweating away on exercise machines, and finally, we reached the Opera House where the doors were just closing. I managed to catch a glimpse of a big poster standing on an easel set up outside the doors saying, "*THE MARRIAGE OF FIGARO.*" My heart flipped as I saw, "Antonio Balboni as Figaro." *That's my uncle*, I thought proudly. An usher pressed a program into our hands and said, "You better hurry."

The lights were dimming as we raced down a red carpet past rows and rows of seats packed with people. The overhead balconies were also packed. It seemed very fancy and grand; the ceiling was incredibly high with paintings of chubby angels flying around fluffy pink clouds in a light blue sky. Our seats were way up in the front, and I felt as if everyone in the whole place must be watching us as we scrambled past people's knees. Mom kept saying, "Sorry, sorry, sorry," over and over again, and just as we sank into our seats the house lights went down. Merla, Tony's girlfriend, who had a seat next to Mom's, beamed and nodded her long hair and dangly earrings at us.

A spotlight found the conductor in the orchestra pit, and then he raised his baton and the music began. Well, I thought, here goes.

The Marriage of Figaro has *four* acts. I didn't know if I would be able to stand it. But to my surprise, the overture made me think of horses racing across a pasture and jumping over fences. And then I noticed Marisa sitting two seats to my right in the row in front of us. Good grief! That girl was haunting me. She was sitting next to a woman who was wearing a gauzy silver dress. I could only see her bony shoulders and the back of her long, thin neck. Her white hair was done up like a dancer's. I figured she must be Madame Petrovna. I remembered Marisa's note to Quentin. Madame Petrovna was going to give Marisa some kind of clue tonight. And then the man sitting next to Madame Petrovna caught my eye.

He was wearing a rumpled, gray sweatshirt, and he had a whole bunch of messy, gray hair. Well, I thought, *he* sure didn't get dressed up to go to the opera, but then, in the hood of the sweatshirt, I caught sight of a pointy nose . . . and then whiskers . . . and then . . . beady little eyes. I leaned forward to get a closer look Yep. There was a mouse, all right, hiding in the hood of that man's sweatshirt.

The overture ended, everyone clapped, and then the

huge, cranberry-red, velvety curtains on the stage parted. I caught my breath, and Mom squeezed my arm. The first person we saw was Tony dressed up like a bullfighter. He strode across the stage carrying a yardstick and singing numbers in Italian at the top of his lungs. I'd heard Tony rehearsing this opening song a hundred times, but it was different now that it was for real.

As the opera got going, something was always happening. People were constantly hiding behind chairs or curtains or in closets and jumping in and out of windows. It wouldn't have been that boring to watch if I could have concentrated, but I kept being distracted by the mouse. Every time someone sang one of those songs they call "arias" in an opera, that mouse closed its eyes and started swaying along with the music. I was about to nudge Mom and show her, but just as Tony was launching into another song, he *croaked*.

The mouse's eyes flew open; Mom grabbed my arm; Merla grabbed *her* arm. The entire audience sat up. For a split second there was terrible silence. Then the orchestra picked up the tune, and Tony started singing again. He seemed to be going along okay, and everybody, all together at the same time, breathed out one huge sigh of relief. The mouse, too, had gone back to swaying, but then Tony croaked again. The orchestra started playing like mad, trying to cover up for him, and then the curtains came down, the lights came up, and it was intermission.

The mouse darted back into the bottom of the hood during the awkward applause. I heard the rumpled man say, "Alas, poor Antonio Balboni."

Mom and Merla were halfway out of their seats. "Should we go and talk to him?" Mom asked.

"Yes," said Merla. "Definitely." Mom turned to me. "We'll

be right back, sweetie. We're going to go down to see Tony."
She and Merla looked so worried; I felt worried, too, and
scared. It must be awful to croak in front of all those people.

I went out to find a bathroom and stood in line. *Everyone*
was talking about Tony. Some were saying they would be
asking to get their money back. It made me feel sick to my
stomach. As I was coming out of the bathroom, I saw Marisa
and Madame Petrovna. Marisa was wearing a shimmer-
ing, yellow dress and she looked like a butterfly. Madame
Petrovna, in her silver dress, looked like a moth. She was
leaning on Marisa's arm, walking slowly. I ducked behind a
post in the hallway, hoping they wouldn't see me.

10

Peeking around from behind the post, I could see that Madame Petrovna had a white face with bright red, round spots of rouge on her cheeks. Her eyes were outlined with black mascara, and she was wearing bright red lipstick. She looked like a doll.

"Where is Felix?" asked Madame Petrovna peevishly, and then her face lit up. "Ah, there he is."

The man with the messy gray hair in the rumpled sweatshirt came up to them. The front of the shirt said I LIKE CHEESE in big letters.

"I've decided to take Charles home," said Felix. "Tomorrow is a very important day for him. It's the National Mouse Competition, and I'm afraid he's been rather upset by tonight's performance and may have trouble getting to sleep. Dear ladies, Charles and I shall be saying good evening to you." Felix bowed to Madame Petrovna and Marisa.

Madame Petrovna put a hand on his arm. "Wait, Felix. Explain to the child."

A slow smile spread across Felix's face. "Ah," he said, "I've been working for years on developing a special electronic signal that stimulates the part of the brain that controls language. With the latest in laser technology, I'm halfway there with Charles. But you see, my dear, in the end, it is gold that will do the trick." His voice rose with excitement. "Gold is the best conductor of electronics. If I could get my hands on enough of it, it would improve my use of laser beams tenfold. I could get the monochromatic, single-phase columnated light leaving the ruby through a half-*gold* mirror instead of silver and then the language part of Charles's brain would be stimulated for sure. Have him *talking*. Using human speech!"

He bowed again and then shuffled off down the hall.

Madame Petrovna swiveled her head on her long neck and gazed after him. "He is a genius—a genius," she exclaimed. "If we can do this for him, Marrrisa . . ." She sure could roll her r's. She tucked a stray strand of hair back into her bun. "Now then . . ." She leaned toward Marisa, and I thought for sure she was about to tell her the clue, but then she hesitated, saying, "Come along, my dear. Let's find a spot that is not so crowded." Together the two of them fluttered off down the hall.

If I were going to find the gold before Marisa did, there was no time to lose. I decided that since I was in the east wing, Rosie could run me up to the 15th floor right now, and I could have a look around. There were so many people milling about, it took me awhile to weave past them to get to the bank of elevators. As the elevator doors opened, there was Rosie sitting on her stool, knitting away. The pink thing she'd been knitting had grown a lot longer since the last time I'd seen it.

"Aiden, dolling, how nice to see you," she said as I stepped in. "Are you here by yourself?"

"Mom and I came to see Tony in his opera, but I'd like to go up to the 15th floor for a minute, please," I said.

Just as the doors were about to close, Felix Brown stuck himself in between them. "Home, Rosie," he said. "We must go home, Charles and I."

"Surely the opera isn't over!" Rosie exclaimed.

"Ah," said Felix with a groan, "for us, this evening, it is over, indeed. Take us home. Charles must get his beauty sleep. The National Mouse Competition is tomorrow."

Rosie nodded. "That's right. It's being held right here in the ballroom, isn't it?"

Charles suddenly peeked out of the neckband of Felix's sweatshirt. He stared at me with large, glowing, brown eyes. Then he popped all the way out and ran down the whole length of Felix's body and onto the floor. He sat there, nose and whiskers quivering, larger and a lot cuter than the mice I'd seen around the house and the barn. He was white, with dark eye-patches around his dark eyes, and his bottom half looked as if it had been dipped in black paint.

"Charles!" Felix exclaimed. "Whatever are you doing?"

"Perhaps he knows that Tony Balboni is Aiden's uncle," Rosie suggested, as the doors shut, "and he wants to be close to someone related to the great man."

"Antonio Balboni is your *uncle*?" Felix looked at me in astonishment while Charles squeaked excitedly. He started running in circles around my feet.

"Charles admires your uncle so very much," said Felix.

As I bent down and put out a finger, Charles stopped running. I lightly touched the top of his head. "Nice to meet you, Charles," I said. Charles sat up, holding his paws up in front of him. I almost expected him to reach up and shake my hand.

"I think you've made his day," said Felix as Rosie stopped the elevator and opened the doors. "And I do hope the rest of the opera goes better for your poor uncle." Felix scooped Charles into one large hand, bowed, and stepped out of the elevator.

It was the 15th floor, so I stepped out with them. As they went off down the hallway, I realized I didn't have the slightest idea where to go next. I didn't even know what I was looking for. This treasure hunt wasn't going to be so easy. I walked past a bunch of doors and then realized with a rush of panic that I had to get back to the opera.

Rosie took me back down to the lobby, and I dashed out of the elevator. The doors to the Opera House were shut tight when I got there. An usher in a white blouse and black skirt was standing in front of the door. "Sorry," she said, frowning sternly at me, "you'll just have to wait for the next intermission. Can't have you coming in now. It'll be another half an hour at least."

Oh, good grief, I thought. Mom was going to be so mad at me. I turned and slowly walked back to Rosie's elevator.

"Oh hello," said Rosie in surprise when she saw me again.
"I didn't get back in time after the intermission," I said. "I have to wait for the next one and Mom will be upset."

"My nephew's wife, Edna, is at the door," said Rosie. "I'll just have a word with her. She'll let you back in."

"Oh no, please," I said. "That would be so embarrassing. We're sitting so close to the front."

Rosie tilted her head, considering. "Well, how about I get my nephew, Fred—he's one of the ushers who stands in the back—to get word to your mum that you're safe with me. He'll know who she is—known her since forever. You just sit over there and rest easy until you have to get back." She pointed to a chair in the corner of the elevator. "You and I can have a nice, quiet chat while I work on my baby blanket for Minnie—she's our youngest grandchild, you know, who works over in number 20, and she's due to have our ninth great-grandchild any minute."

I sat down in Rosie's chair. I was thinking I should ask her what she remembered about the treasure hunt. But just then a broad, beefy man in the Ingle Building uniform walked up. "Came to tell you Minnie's gone to the hospital," he said in a gruff voice.

"Oh, Grip! Oh my goodness!" Rosie exclaimed.

Grip folded his arms tightly against his chest. "And I might as well tell you now, I'm using this as an opportunity to move Ernie into her elevator."

Rosie rose off her stool, letting the knitting slip to the floor. "You're not making Ernie go into number 20! Why, Ernie has been Mrs. Ingle's operator in number 10 forever, long before you even thought of being born!"

"Complaints have been made," said Grip with a stony expression. "Rudeness to the clientele."

Rosie put her hands on her hips. "And since when do *you* get to make decisions like this?"

"Management made me the boss, remember?" Grip said. He unfolded his arms and yanked at the brim of his cap.

"Does Ernie know about this yet?" Rosie asked.

"Telling him as soon as his shift is over," said Grip, looking at his watch.

He turned on his heels and marched away.

Rosie sat down heavily on her stool. I reached down and picked up the knitting.

"Thanks, dolling," she said as she gathered it back and stuffed it into a large knitting bag. She had tears in her eyes. She reached over and pressed the button that closed the doors. "Don't want that sneak eavesdropping on me again. He keeps popping out of the woodwork like some sort of troll. Mrs. Ingle has taken a shine to him—can't for the life of me figure out why." She suddenly grabbed my arm. "Aiden, dolling, do you think you can do something for me? Could you go over and give a message to Ernie? I'd go myself, but

I'll lose my job for sure if I leave my post. First, tell him what Grip said. About moving him to number 20."

"You want *me* to tell him?" I stared at Rosie in disbelief.

"I know, dolling, it's hard—but you being a Balboni and all, why, I feel like you're practically family. Mr. Balboni was so kind to us when we first came here from the Old Country, he really was." Rosie seemed lost in thought for a moment and then said, "Oh, my word. I know what we'll do." She dug into her knitting bag and brought out a key. "Give him this and tell him it's time. Tell him to collect it all." She pressed the key into the palm of my hand and curled my fingers over it. "He's in number 10, right off the main lobby. But mind, don't say a word if anyone else is around, especially that snoop!" she finished with a splutter.

I hesitated for a moment, wondering just how much time had gone by. Could I get over to Ernie's elevator and still be back for the next intermission? Then I figured Rosie really needed me to do this.

I took off at a run, loping through corridors, through the lobby of the east wing, and finally through the glass doors until I came to the main lobby, which was even fancier than the lobby in the east wing.

Darting through a crowd of tourists standing around with suitcases, I sped into another small hallway with a bank of elevators on each side. I joined the waiting people gathered there and began to worry about how I would break the news to Ernie.

"Are you coming in or what?" A gruff voice broke into my thoughts, and I barely managed to jump into the elevator just as the doors were closing.

It was Ernie at the controls. I had met him a couple of

times when Mom and I had come to hear Tony sing at the Ingle Building Opera House. I doubted he remembered me. He was as thin as Rosie was round. His uniform seemed two sizes too big for him, and his hat hung down over his face so you could barely see his soupy, gray eyes.

"Where to, ladies and gentlemen?" he asked mournfully. A white mustache drooped over the corners of his mouth.

I wasn't sure what to say, but I knew I had to stay put until everyone was out so I could talk to Ernie privately.

"I'm going to the top," I said, feeling myself turn red as everyone in the elevator stared at me.

There was an awkward silence as we went up. No one was looking at me anymore but at the floor or up at the ceiling or at the grandfather clock. I remembered that clock now. No chandelier hung in here but almost more amazing was the big grandfather clock bolted to the back wall. It was fancier than the clock we had at home or the one at East Park. Painted above the dial was a mountain, and the mountaintop was covered with gold snow. I remembered Pops studying it and asking Ernie a million questions about how it could keep running smoothly with the elevator going up and down all the time.

After a while, I was the only one left in the elevator. I cleared my throat a few times, but I was too nervous to blurt out the bad news. At the 86th floor, Ernie stopped the elevator and opened the doors. "All out what's gettin' out," he said glumly.

"Is this the top floor?" I asked.

"Top floor is the Eyrie."

"The—the what?"

"Don't you know what an eyrie is?"

"It's—a place that's high up—where eagles or falcons live—"

"That's right, little lady, very good. And that's where Mrs. Ingle lives. And no one goes there. So, if you're getting off, here's the place to do it."

"I want to go back down to the lobby," I said.

"Think I have nothing better to do than stand around and cart you up and down the Ingle Building?" Ernie's mustache drooped even more. He pressed the button and glared at me gloomily.

"I just came from Rosie," I said, clearing my throat again. "Maybe you remember me? I'm Tony Balboni's niece—Allegra Balboni's daughter—"

Ernie's expression completely changed. "Ah, that explains it. Thought you looked familiar. Well." He put a hand on my shoulder. "I heard about your loss. That's real sad. I only met your father a few times, but I liked him."

My eyes filled with tears for a moment. "Thanks," I said. Then I swallowed hard. "I have a message for you from Rosie. She said to tell you Minnie just went into the hospital."

Ernie looked pleased. "Well, that's something."

I took a breath. "And she said Grip wants to move you into her elevator."

"He said *that*!" Ernie whipped off his cap. Little strands of white hair were pressed against his scalp.

"And Rosie said to tell you it's, um, time. To collect it all. And to give you this." I held the key out to Ernie.

Ernie took the key from me and with a shaking hand managed to put it into his pocket. "She's right," he said quietly.

The doors to the lobby opened. I wanted to rush out of

there, but there was an old lady, even older than Ernie, blocking the way. I realized with a start that she was Mrs. Ingle. The prettiest woman I had ever seen was standing beside her. She had shoulder-length dark hair, beautiful, dark skin, and large, dark eyes. Mrs. Ingle was leaning on her arm.

"Mrs. Ingle," said Ernie, putting his cap back on, "is the opera over already?"

"Left early," Mrs. Ingle sniffed. "Something's the matter with Antonio Balboni's voice. Couldn't bear to listen to another note."

Oh, poor Tony, I thought, as I stood staring at Mrs. Ingle. She was wearing a white suit. Her white hair had been permed into tight little curls. Her eyes were the cold blue of a winter sky and flashed like the diamonds in her ears. She reminded me of an icicle.

"How much of the opera is left?" I asked nervously.

Mrs. Ingle turned, looking startled. "Patsy—? How—?"

"N-no," I said, "I'm—not—"

"It's all right, Mrs. Een-go-lee," the woman with her said. Her accent was just like Fernando Costa's, our taxi driver. She took Mrs. Ingle gently by the arm and guided her into the elevator.

"Forgive me," Mrs. Ingle said. She was trembling slightly. "For a moment I thought—you look just like—oh, I'm an old woman, never mind, pay no attention to me." She sank into the chair that was at the back corner of the elevator and then, reaching out, patted the grandfather clock. "It's still working, isn't it, Ernie? You see that the clock man comes in regularly, don't you? Keeps it wound?"

Ernie sagged more than ever. "How can I, when you're moving me out of this elevator—I won't be able to look after your clock."

"I'm so tired, Ernie," said Mrs. Ingle, cutting him off. "Please get me back upstairs. I must check on my birds."

The pretty woman raised her shoulders slightly at Ernie as if to say she was sorry. Ernie grunted angrily and pressed a button, and the elevator went on its way. I turned and ran as fast as I could back to the east wing. The doors to the opera house were open now, and a wave of people came swirling into the lobby.

And there was Mom, looking pinched and anxious, clutching my raincoat and standing with Merla in the middle of the lobby.

"Mom!" I said, pushing past people to get to her.

"Oh my gosh, Aiden," she said, her face relaxing but her eyes brimming with tears. "What have you been doing?"

Peering over the edge of my bed, I saw that Mom was awake, reading. She waved to me and then put a finger to her lips, pointing toward Tony's bedroom.

Last night he and Mom and Merla had stayed up late talking about what had happened. I heard bits and pieces of what they were saying. Tony was petrified he was bombing out of his career. He was worried about paying back loans he'd taken out to study at an opera school in Italy. I kept hearing the word *debt*. I shivered. I *hated* that word with its silent "b" in the middle of it, silent like a heart you didn't know was bad.

After Pops died, Mom sold some of the heifers and young calves, some of the tractors, and even a parcel of land. I kept hearing her say things like, "The cost of grain and the taxes have quadrupled," and I wondered sometimes if that's why Pops had had a heart attack, because keeping up the farm had just been too much.

I got up and sat on the couch and did homework for awhile. Then I remembered it was a long weekend—no school on Monday—I could save some of the homework until later. Time to get out of that stuffy apartment.

"I'm going out to the park, and then I'm going to meet a boy in my class named Adam later," I whispered.

Mom's face lit up. I knew she was pleased I was making friends.

On my way out the door Henrietta slipped past me. She ran down the stairs and I ran after her. I thought I'd be able to catch her at the bottom where the mailboxes were, but someone opened the door to the building right at that moment and she darted outside.

"Henrietta!" I screamed, but she had already run down the steps to the sidewalk. Ears twitching, she waited a moment and then sped across the street. She made it across, and then I couldn't believe it. Black Jack popped through the fence that ran around the outside of the park. The two cats touched noses and then disappeared back through the fence.

By the time I ran across the street and into the park, they were nowhere to be seen. "You better come back!" I called out. "And Black Jack, you'd better take care of her!"

"Who are you talking to?" It was Quentin. And just behind him was Marisa.

"My imaginary friend, Abigail," I said. If they thought I was weird, well, I *would* be weird. That was Liesl's strategy, right?

"Oh, is she helping your uncle sing better?" Marisa asked with a sarcastic smile.

How did she know Tony was my uncle? I wanted to slug Marisa, I really did.

"Come on, Marisa, if we're going to the Ingle Building, let's go," said Quentin.

I felt myself turn cold as I watched them leave. So they were on their way. As I stood there fuming, wishing I were going with Adam right now, a soccer ball came rolling toward me.

"Mine," a little boy, about four years old, called out.

"Okay," I said. I kicked it back to him.

"Nice kick!" A tall man with a shaved head was standing with the little boy. When he smiled at me, a gold front tooth flashed in the sun. I looked at him more closely.

"You drove us last night! When you picked up the bird that was hurt!"

Fernando broke into a huge grin. "I remember—you and your mother were going to hear the opera—I hope I didn't make you late."

The little boy kicked the ball back to me.

"Way to go, Beckham," I said, booting it back.

"Hey, you put some spin on that!" Fernando exclaimed with a huge grin. "You play *futebol, né?*"

"Football?"

"What you call soccer," he said.

"I'm really bad at soccer," I said.

Fernando frowned. "What makes you say that? You got something natural! You like to learn a little? I give you some pointers. Me, I am Fernando Costa, and this is my little boy, Melo."

"I'm Aiden Farmer," I said.

"Nice to meet you, Aiden. Here, look, try this." He dribbled the ball over in front of me. "All right, Aiden, try grazing the ball low on the far side of it—like this." He showed me in slow motion, not actually touching the ball. Then he took a few steps back and running for it kicked for real. The ball rose up in a curvy arc. "You try now," he said, bringing the ball back and plunking it down in front of me.

I ran for the ball and my foot missed it completely. I ended up flat on my back. Melo laughed his head off.

"Hush, Melo, it's not kind to laugh," said Fernando, but he was laughing, too, in a way that made me not mind.

"Try once more. Point your toe a bit more."

This time the ball lifted off. "Very good!" Fernando ran right over and high-fived me.

People suddenly began to gather, carrying portable chairs and blankets, chattering in different languages, unpacking big baskets. Athletes filled the field, doing all these fancy dribbles, heading the ball, passing.

"What's going on?" I asked.

"We *imgrantes* have soccer games here in Gill Park every Sunday."

Melo started clinging to Fernando's leg. "I want to play, too," he said.

"You *can't* Melo, you will get trampled," said Fernando, exasperated. "Ah, I wish my wife, Ana, could be here, but she is working."

"I'll watch him," I said. "Come on, Melo, we'll find a ball and play our own game."

Melo unlatched himself from Fernando and flung himself at me. "Yes!" he shouted happily. He grabbed on to one of my hands.

Fernando's gold-toothed grin lit up his face. He let the ball he had been carrying drop to the ground. "You can use this," he said and, making a fist, touched my arm gratefully with his knuckles. "*Obrigado*—thank you with all my heart!" He loped off down to the field.

"Kick to me!" Melo ordered.

Melo and I played for a while, making a goal out of his

jacket and mine, and soon he was perfectly happy to sit in my lap on the sidelines and watch the game. It was amazing to watch. It looked like a professional game.

And then suddenly Melo scrambled off my lap and said, "I want to play with papa!"

"Oh, Melo, you can't. Come on, you and I will play again," I said.

Melo broke away from me and kicked the ball as hard as he could toward the playing field.

"Hey, Melo, hey, buddy!"

A tall, lanky woman with long, white hair intercepted the ball. She was wearing a black T-shirt with a picture of a hawk on the front of it and jeans.

"Bird Lady!" cried Melo, his tantrum forgotten.

13

I looked at the Bird Lady curiously. "Are you the one fixing up Lady Peregrine?"

"Yes," she said. "She's in shock, poor thing. Damaged wing. Later when she's feeling better, I'll trying imping on new feathers, but she needs a few days to recover. Now," she said, turning to Melo, "maybe I could tell you a story."

"Yes, right now," he said, tugging on her hand. "Tell me a story."

She sat down, patting the ground. "All right then, sit," she said. "You're welcome, too," she said to me. I sat down with Melo in my lap, relieved that he was being distracted. "This is a story my father used to tell me."

"Once there was a girl," the Bird Lady began. "She lived with her mama and papa in a farmhouse on the top of the hill." Melo sat quietly now, with his thumb in his mouth. "And the girl often lay on her back looking up at the clouds dreaming of castles. How, she thought, she would like to be a princess living in a castle."

Melo was quiet and still as the Bird Lady told the story.

"One day, the girl was feeding the chickens when she

heard the little ants who were scurrying in the corn call to her. 'You must go now,' they said."

The Bird Lady spoke in a little voice, and both Melo and I laughed.

"The girl wondered where the ants were telling her to go, but later, as she was digging in the garden to weed the potatoes, the grass cried out, 'Go and find the gold.'"

Find the gold. I felt prickles up and down my neck. I stared at the Bird Lady.

"And that evening," the Bird Lady went on, "as the girl was splitting wood, she heard the clouds say, 'Go and climb the mountain.'

"The girl looked out into the far distance and saw the mountain she had looked at every day of her life. The bare, rocky top was shining in the sun. 'That must be the mountain,' she said. 'That must be where the ants and the grass and the clouds are telling me to go. That must be where the gold is. And if I find it, I shall be able to build myself a castle.'

"Very early the next morning, the girl left the farmhouse even before her mother and father were awake. She walked all day until she came to the base of the mountain. There seemed to be more than one path leading to the top, and the girl was not sure which one to climb. But then she heard a little ant voice say, 'Make your own path.'

"The girl climbed and she climbed—" and here the Bird Lady stopped and thought for a moment—"I am trying to remember how many steps she climbed—ah, yes, 151." Melo smiled with his thumb stuck into his mouth. "My father always used to say, remember the number, it's important!

"So—as the girl finished the 151st step, she looked around and saw ugly, twisty trees, and she was worried she was lost. But just as she was thinking this, a handsome man wearing a three-piece suit popped up right in her path. He was a troll, but the girl didn't realize it because she didn't know trolls could be so good-looking."

A *troll*! I stared at the Bird Lady. *Was* this the story Leo had told me about?

"'I'm here to recommend a different path than the one you're on,' said the troll in a buttery voice. 'If you go up *that* way,' and he pointed with a very clean, un-troll-like fingernail, 'you can get the kind of gold that pays for castles. Haven't you always dreamed of living in a castle?'

"'Oh yes,' said the girl.

"She started running up the path, so excited was she, but the blades of grass tickled her ankles and said, 'Make your own path.' The girl stepped off the path the troll had told her to follow and started blazing her own trail again. This time she walked exactly 303 steps."

"Three hundred and three," said Melo through his thumb.

A little ant ran across my hand. *Oh my gosh*, I thought, brushing the ant away. *All these funny numbers—I have to remember them.*

The Bird Lady pulled back her long hair, turning it into a ponytail, and went on. "The twisty trees that grew on the mountain were getting smaller, and the rocks she had to scramble over were getting more jagged, and the air was getting thinner, and it was getting harder and harder to breathe. And by and by, the girl noticed it was getting quiet. Not a twitter of a bird. Not a crick of a cricket. Just quiet. Until a shrill voice called out, 'IF YOU'RE LOOKING FOR GOLD, YOU BETTER GET ON A DIFFERENT PATH!'"

The Bird Lady raised her voice and shouted, and Melo giggled happily. And just then the pretty woman who had been with Mrs. Ingle the night before came and sat down with us. She stared at me, saying, "You're the girl in the elevator!" Melo said, "Shh, Mama," and the Bird Lady nodded, saying, "Hello, Ana," and Melo crawled into her lap. "Keep going, Bird Lady," he said.

"The girl turned around and perched on the top of a twisted old tree was a glamorous young woman wearing a shiny blue dress. She had long black hair and high heels. Even though it was very odd for someone so dressed up to be sitting in a tree, she was so glamorous the girl did not even think twice about it. She, too, was a troll, of course. 'We've been expecting you, but you better listen to me, my good friend.' The troll wasn't shouting anymore but sort of purring. 'You can't go up just any path. If it's a castle you're wanting, castle gold is up THAT path,' and the troll pointed a long, pink fingernail at a big, wide path that looked easy to climb.

"The girl started to climb the big, wide path, but the clouds overhead darkened and sent down stinging hailstones. 'Get back on your own path right now,' the clouds yelled at her.

"The girl could take a hint, all right, so she stepped back onto her own path. And she started climbing again. She climbed and she climbed 1,114 steps."

Melo laughed again at the funny number, and I told myself, *1,114*, you better remember that.

"Now the sun was beginning to set, but she could see she did not have very far to go for just a few feet away was the top of the mountain. She ran the last little bit. And there, at last, lying all around her feet were the gleaming nuggets of gold. She bent down and began picking them up. 'Five should be enough to build a castle,' she thought.

"But as she began to climb down the mountain, she heard, 'HA HA HA, HEE HEE HEE, YOU WILL NEVER TAKE OUR GOLD!'

"The girl suddenly saw trolls everywhere, not at all handsome and pretty and polished, but warty and bumpy and slimy and grimy. 'No!' they were screeching. 'No, no, you can't, you can't, you can't take our gold, our gold, our gold, no, no, no, no, you can't, you can't, take our gold!'

"Closer and closer they came to the girl, drawing the ring in tighter and tighter. But just in time, the little ants stung the trolls' feet and they tumbled in somersaults down the side of the mountain. They landed in a patch of tall grass, in tangles so thick they couldn't move. And then a whole fleet of black clouds moved in and sent lightning bolts at them.

"Those trolls couldn't lift a finger. Those trolls couldn't even open an eyelid. Those trolls were out cold!

"Happy to be safe, the girl ran all the way home.

"'Ma and Pa,' she called as she climbed up her hill, 'Ma and Pa, come see what I have found!'"

There was a roar from the crowd as a goal was made. Everyone was standing and shouting, and it looked as if the game was over. Fernando came striding over to us, shining with sweat, smiling a huge gold-toothed grin. He kissed Ana and lifted Melo off the ground. "Good game, great game!" he shouted.

In the middle of this, my cell phone rang. "Hey," said Adam, "I'm here at the fountain waiting for you."

"I'll be there in five," I said.

I looked around frantically for the Bird Lady. I wanted to hear the ending of the story, and I wanted to ask her who she was, but she had disappeared.

14

I ran as fast as I could to the fountain.

Adam stood next to it with shoulders hunched and hands dug into his pockets. His head was tucked into his jacket like a turtle's. "It's beginning to rain," he said. "Maybe we should do this another day."

"No, come on," I said. "Marisa and Quentin are already there. Let's try the bike path—it goes through the woods, and it'll be drier under the trees. Race you there!" I leaped out in front of Adam and started running.

Along the bike path, the rain really wasn't so bad, and it made a nice pattering sound as it came down through the leaves. I kept up a pretty fast clip for quite a while, but I stopped as Black Jack suddenly darted across the path in front of me. He stopped, too, and turned and stared at us, his yellow eyes bright and unblinking.

Adam came up, holding his side and breathing hard. "That's supposed to be bad luck, a black cat crossing your path."

"Jack is *good* luck." I put out my hand, and Jack came up and rubbed against it. "But where's Henrietta?" I asked.

Black Jack stretched his neck and then bounded away

and disappeared into a ditch that ran alongside the bike path. I started running again, hoping to find Henrietta. It wasn't long before we came to Mitch's tree.

"Mitch Bloom has a tree house up there," said Adam.

"I know," I said. "Mitch Bloom is my cousin."

"No way," said Adam. "Have you been up in the elevator?"

"Yesterday."

Adam looked at me with envy. "I'd like to go up there sometime."

I looked up. The oak was huge, and I could only just see the bottom of the house from where I stood. "If you have to live in a city, this sure would be the way to do it. When I find the gold, I'm going to build a tree house at home just like this one."

"*If* you find it," said Adam. "Sure you want to go? It's beginning to rain hard now."

A small tiger-striped face with green eyes appeared out of the grassy bank on the other side of the path for just one second. "Henrietta!" I called, going right over to the spot where I'd seen her. Parting the high grass, I found a hole in the ground.

"It's like a rabbit hole or something," I said. And that's when I saw the wooden door in the side of the bank. It had green mold growing all over it. Unless you were looking for it, you wouldn't notice it. It had a wooden doorknob that turned easily enough, but to open the door all the way I had to give it a yank, as the bottom edge caught against the earth. Peering in, it seemed as if there was a space big enough to stand in. "Come on," I said. "We can get in out of the rain."

"Are you *kidding*? I'm not going in *there*. I'm claustrophobic."

"You can come or not," I said, wishing Blake was with me instead of Adam.

Adam grunted and then came and stood beside me. A little light filtered in from the hole in the top of the bank where Henrietta had popped out.

"I think this is the start of a tunnel," I said. "We could see where it goes."

"Are you *kidding*?" Adam asked again.

"I'm going in," I said. It was scary, all right, but I plunged into the black hole. To my surprise, Adam followed me.

For a while we could walk along just fine, but it was getting darker and then it began to narrow and the ceiling lowered. I got down on my hands and knees and began to crawl. It was really dark now, hold-your-hand-in-front-of-your-face-and-not-see-a-thing dark. It was hot and stuffy, and I was clammy and steamy because I had gotten pretty wet before ducking into the bank. My head brushed against the earth ceiling. I was glad I had on my hat.

"What if this doesn't really go anywhere and we have to crawl out backward because there isn't enough room to turn around in here? Or what if we get stuck or the whole thing caves in?" Adam had a way of voicing all my worries out loud.

"Let's keep going for five more minutes," I said.

We kept crawling. It was hard on the knees and hands and, just as I was regretting the whole thing, I felt my foot being grabbed.

"Someone's in the tunnel," Adam whispered. "Following us. Listen."

I froze, listening, and sure enough, there was a slight rustling, like the sound my jacket was making as it brushed against the sides of the tunnel. "It's probably one of the cats,"

I said, but *rats* was what I was really thinking. Prickles of panic began racing up the back of my neck.

"Too big," he said in a whisper.

Oh good grief, it was a *big* rat, I was sure of it.

The sound came closer and then stopped. "It knows we stopped," Adam whispered. "Try moving again and see what happens."

I put one hand down in front of the other and inched forward. The rustling started again. I stopped, Adam stopped, and the thing behind us stopped.

"Aiden Farmer, I know you're there." A voice broke into the stillness.

"Liesl!" I was so relieved, I almost started crying. I heard her cackle. She came up behind Adam.

"Good grief, Liesl, what are you doing here?"

"Following you. I saw you going into my secret passage."

"*Your* secret passage?"

"Sure, I live right next to it, don't I? And hardly anyone knows about it. I use it all the time to get around. Runs right through the park. Come on, keep going, we're almost through the worst part."

We crawled a few more yards and gradually the solid black of the tunnel turned a filmy gray—a few more feet and there was enough light to see and, finally, enough room to stand up.

"I think we can walk here," I said.

"Course you can. Who is this guy?" asked Liesl.

Adam groaned as he sat up and then stood and stretched. "I should never have come here."

"Aw, come on. This is way better than HAH," I said. "Adam, this is my cousin, Liesl. She lives in the tree house."

"I've seen you in the park," said Adam. "You draw chalk portraits of people. You're pretty good."

"I'm more than pretty good," said Liesl. "I'm—"

"Hey!" Adam grabbed my arm. "There's a door. See, there's light seeping under the crack. Ever hear that expression—there's light at the end of the tunnel?" He started laughing hysterically.

"What's the matter with him?" Liesl asked.

"He's not used to crawling through secret passages," I said, feeling a little hysterical myself.

Adam was ahead of me now. He opened the door, and we found ourselves standing in a brightly lit room. It seemed way too bright after being in all that darkness. Row after row of gray, metal boxes lined the walls.

"Electrical stuff," said Adam.

"Where are we?" I asked Liesl.

"You'll see," she said, looking gleeful.

"In the sewer or something," Adam said, sounding depressed. But then we heard the squawk of a car being unlocked and soon after the sound of a car starting. Adam pushed through the door at the other end of the room, and we followed him into a dimly lit space full of cars.

"Well, we're on the third level of some parking garage," said Adam pointing to a number on a post. "We should remember that if we need to go back through the tunnel again. And the door, too," he added, nodding at the door we'd just come through. It had a sign on it saying, ELECTRICAL. NO ADMITTANCE. "Not that I ever want to go through there again." His shirttails hung down below the bottom of his jacket, his khakis had two brown, round spots on the knees, and his sneakers weren't white anymore. My jeans were dirty, too. I brushed them off, but Liesl, in an old pair of overalls, didn't seem to care one bit about the dirt.

"Come on, let's go," she said impatiently.

We followed her through a door and up a set of stairs, and at the top she pushed open a heavy fire door saying, "Ta da!"

We came out into a big lobby with familiar-looking plush, cranberry-red carpets with yellow falcons woven into them.

"I don't believe it!" Adam and I said at the same time.

"We're right where we wanted to be!" I said.

"Why?" Liesl asked. "Why did you want to be here?"

Adam and I looked at each other.

"Of course you don't have to tell me. I mean, I'm only a removed cousin, and this kid is probably a kissing cousin." The blue vein over the bridge of Liesl's nose began to blaze like a warning sign.

Adam rolled his eyes, tufting up his hair.

"Oh, knock it off, he's not any kind of cousin. He's a friend from school," I said.

"Oh I see," said Liesl, rolling her eyes, "he's from your stuck-up school—now I get it." She started to walk away.

"Just hang on a sec, Liesl," I said. "Don't be so huffy. I haven't even had a chance to tell you anything."

Liesl turned and immediately looking more cheerful said, "Yeah, you're right. I'm working on that. Frankie says the same thing. I'm oversensitive. So, you don't have to tell me if you don't want to."

She seemed like a walking time bomb, but I also remembered how she'd saved my hat from Quentin. Maybe Adam was smart, but Liesl was spunky. She could be a big help. I looked at Adam with raised eyebrows.

"Do what you want. I'm just along for the ride," he said, looking down at his feet.

"We're looking for gold," I said to Liesl.

"Cool," she said. "Where is it? What is it? Pirate treasure?"

"Gold coins," I said. "They're called Gold Falcons. They're hidden somewhere here in the Ingle Building." I took off the hat, pulled back the lining, and pointed to the writing. "And this a clue to where they are."

"Wow—FLY TO E15," said Liesl.

"I think the E in the clue means east wing, 15th floor."

"What are we waiting for? Let's fly!" said Liesl.

"We don't even know where we *are* in the Ingle Building," said Adam.

Looking around, I said, "Hold on—yes, we do—there's the Opera House, so we're already in the east wing."

I walked over to the poster on the easel that stood outside the entrance to the Opera House. Tony's name had been covered over with a card with someone else's name on it. "That's where Uncle Tony usually sings," I said to Liesl as she came over to look. "He's another one of your cousins."

Liesl nodded. "I know, and I heard about what happened."

I tugged at one of the doors, and to my surprise it opened. As my eyes swept over the rows of empty seats leading up to the velvety cranberry-red curtains, I felt terrible. Poor Tony and his croaking.

"Come on, I don't want to be here all day," said Adam. "I still have homework to do."

"I bet you get a lot of stupid homework at your stuck-up school," said Liesl.

"How do you know it's stuck-up?" asked Adam.

"I know things," said Liesl, lifting her chin slightly.

"We'll go up in my friend Rosie's elevator," I said, breaking into their bickering.

We headed for the little hallway with a bank of elevators on each side. A few minutes later, the doors opened, and we saw the chandelier swaying slightly as it hung from the middle of the ceiling of the elevator, the crystals sparkling and dancing with rainbows.

"Aiden, dolling! Got your old-timer's cap on again, I see. Very nice," Rosie exclaimed. Lowering her voice, she said, "I think you saved Ernie's life last night, dolling, by letting him know the bad news in advance. By the time Grip got to him, he was able to hold himself together. And believe you me, we're making *plans*." In a more normal tone of voice, she asked, "And how's Tony doing, dolling? I heard all about it— I'm so sorry he's having trouble with his voice. And where are you and your friends going today?"

Before we could tell her, Felix Brown in his rumpled I LOVE CHEESE sweatshirt stepped into the elevator. "Rosie, my dear," he said, grinning from ear to ear, "what a day! What a day! This morning, Charles won best in show for Dutch Marked Mice!"

"Congratulations, what wonderful news, Felix!" said Rosie, beaming.

"That's great news about Charles," I said.

"Ah, the niece of the great Antonio Balboni," said Felix. "Once again we meet."

The letters of I LOVE CHEESE rippled a bit, and Charles's head appeared out of the front of the sweatshirt. Liesl squealed with delight, and Adam took a step back.

Felix rubbed his hands together. "And we are getting closer and closer, Rosie, to the day when Charles can speak his own mind."

"Imagine!" Rosie exclaimed. "The first talking mouse right here in the Ingle Building!" Liesl's eyes widened, and Adam started to grin. "And here, everyone, is the 15th floor. You have reached your destination. Bye-bye, Charles," she said, waving to him, "have a nice day—"

Felix and Charles stepped out, and we followed.

"And I hope your uncle and his voice are on the mend today," said Felix pleasantly as he turned and walked down the hall, Charles on his shoulder.

We stared after them for a moment. "I'd like to hear that mouse talk," said Adam. "But now what? Where do we go?"

"I don't know," I admitted. "Maybe we just start—" but Felix was lumbering back down the hall, shouting, "Charles! Come back here!"

A second later, the black-and-white mouse streaked past us.

"Catch him," Felix cried out in a panic.

We sprinted after Charles as he zipped down the long hallway. On and on he went, under a set of fire doors and then down another long hallway. He stopped, finally, pressing himself against the door of an apartment, his little sides heaving in and out as if he'd just run a marathon.

"Charles," Felix said as he finally caught up to us. He bent over and picked him up. "What were you thinking? Winning best in show must have gone to your head. Thank you very much," he said to us and then lumbered his way back up the hall, muttering to Charles the whole way.

"Okay," said Adam, "now that we're halfway across the building—"

"Wait a minute," I said. We were standing in front of apartment number—151 "steps," I said aloud.

"What are you talking about?" asked Adam.

"There's something on the very bottom of this door," said Liesl suddenly. She knelt down. "Look! There's a tiny drawing of a bird with big wings!"

Both Adam and I dropped to the floor. There *was* a little drawing, a cartoon, really, of a bird facing front with a big belly and drooping wings.

"There's a number on its front," said Adam.

"It's pretty faded," said Liesl. "I can't tell if it's a three or an eight."

"It's a three," I said. I took off the hat and kissed it. "Leo was right!" I shouted. "And the story was right! Come on, let's go to the third floor!"

Taking the elevator closest to us, we met a new operator, but he looked so much like Rosie that after telling him we wanted to go to the third floor, I blurted out, "You must be related to Rosie!"

"My older sister," the man acknowledged.

"How many of you are there?" I asked.

"Well, let's see," he said, holding up a gloved hand. He began counting off on his fingers. "There's Rosie, and then me—I'm Stan—and then Marty, Adele, Dorota, and Boris. And every one of us runs an elevator! How about that! Here's the third floor."

"Come on," Liesl grabbed me by the arm and pulled me out of the elevator.

Adam was already halfway down the hall, but he stopped suddenly. "Do we know where we're going? We don't have Charles this time to show us." Then he stopped for a moment, scratching his head. "And *did* he show us? Or was that just a coincidence?"

"Hang on," I said. I closed my eyes and put my fingers up in the air. "Mr. Ingle . . . is . . . speaking to me. He . . . is . . . telling me apartment number 303."

"*What?*" Adam stared at me. "Are you *crazy*, Aiden?"

As soon as we reached apartment number 303, we dropped down and started looking along the bottom edge of the door. "It's here," Liesl squealed. "I found it!" There was another little, fat cartoon bird at the bottom of the door. She gave me a funny look. "Are you psychic or something?"

I closed my eyes and put two fingers up to my temples. "I am in touch with Edward Ingle," I said mysteriously.

Adam poked me. "Come on, really, how'd you know?"

"Really," I said, "Mr. Ingle and I are in touch."

Adam rolled his eyes, but Liesl was saying, "There are two little marks on its belly."

Adam and I squatted down to look. "It's the number 11," said Adam.

We scrambled to our feet.

"So we go to the 11th floor," said Adam. "And then what? What is Mr. Ingle telling you now?"

I closed my eyes again. "Apartment number . . ." and I paused, pretending to be waiting for the message, "1,114."

"Get out of here!" Adam exclaimed.

"You'll see," I said.

As we waited for the elevator, Adam said, "If I were making up a hunt, I'd make it with algebraic equations."

"And that would be soo much fun," said Liesl, rolling her eyes.

An elevator arrived. It was Stan's again. "You know," he

said as we stepped in, "I'm pretty sure I forgot to mention Stefan." He waved his hands in the air. "We are *always* forgetting Stefan!"

"Can you go to the 11th floor, please," we said.

At the door of apartment number 1,114, we didn't find a thing.

"Hoist me up," said Liesl, "and I'll look at the top." I bent down, lacing my fingers together to make a step. Liesl stuck one foot in and with Adam helping to hold her we managed to hike her up.

"Nothing," she said as she jumped back down.

The three of us sat on the floor, stumped. I was glad no one was out and about in the hallway because it wouldn't have been that easy to explain what we were doing.

"Where is that old Mr. Ingle when you need him?" Adam asked.

We trudged back down the hallway and called for Rosie's elevator. When the doors opened, Marisa, Quentin, and Madame Petrovna were standing beneath the chandelier.

"Ack!" Adam exclaimed, without meaning to.

"Ack is right," said Quentin. Then his eyes widened as he recognized Liesl. So did Marisa's.

"What are *you* doing here?" Marisa asked, making a terrible face. "Frankie isn't here, is she?"

Liesl put her hands on her hips. "What's it to you?"

"More frrriends of yours, Marrrisa, coming to help?" Madame Petrovna smiled a pleasant, lipsticky smile at us.

"No!" Marisa snapped. "We don't need help."

"Yes, you do," said Adam between his teeth. "You need all the help you can get."

"Here's the lobby, dollings," said Rosie. "Lovely to see everyone."

"Ta ta," said Marisa, wafting out of the elevator.

"They're looking for the gold, too," I explained to Liesl.

"What, those wimps?" Liesl put back her head and laughed.

"Looking for gold?" Rosie asked. "Are you—"

But before she could finish asking, a little girl zoomed into the elevator and threw her arms around Rosie.

"Great-Gammy!" she exclaimed. A man and a woman came in and kissed Rosie, too.

"Helloooohh, Miss Vicky Sweetie Pie," Rosie said, singing out the name. "How are we today?"

"I lost a toof last night, Great-Gammy," said the little girl, pointing to a gap in the front of her mouth.

"Well, well, well," said Rosie. She dipped her hand into her knitting bag and came up with a dollar bill. "We'll just have to help out the tooth fairy, won't we?"

"Fank oo," said Vicky.

"Family," Rosie explained to us proudly.

"We went and saw all the mices," said Vicky. "And we wanted to see you and Grampy, too."

Rosie frowned. "Ernie's no longer in number 10, you know. He's been moved to Minnie's elevator."

Vicky's parents looked shocked. "But Gran," said the mom, "he's always been in elevator 10."

"Management has its own ideas," said Rosie, biting her lip.

"Oh my gosh! This is terrible. We'll go see him right now," said the dad. "And then we'll come back and pick you up to take you over to see Minnie and the baby."

"Yes indeed!" Rosie was beaming now.

"Bye-bye, Great-Gammy," said Vicky, hugging Rosie again.

"Bye, dollings," said Rosie to her family. As they left, she sat staring off into space. "Funny to think of Ernie way over on the west wing now," she said sadly. "But not for long . . . not for long! Now, about the gold—" There was a *bing* as someone on another floor called for her. "Come back later and talk to me about the treasure hunt," she said.

As we stepped into the hallway, Adam slapped his forehead.

"The west wing!" he exclaimed. "Of course! We've only been looking in the east wing!"

I could have hugged Adam. "Oh! Adam, you're so smart!"

Adam grinned for a minute, showing the gap between his teeth. Then he said, "Where did we find that first little drawing?"

"On the bottom of the door," I said.

"Yeah, but where—left, right, or middle?"

"On the right," said Liesl.

Adam nodded. "And the next one was too, but that last one was way over on the left. Don't you see?" he asked. "Right side is east; left is west."

"Oh yeah, I'm sure you're right!" I punched the air, excited. "Let's go over to the west wing!"

"Look," said Adam. Tugging on his hair, he shifted from foot to foot. "I can come back tomorrow and start looking again, but I have to go home now."

"*What?*" Liesl exploded. "You're *quitting?*"

"I'm not quitting," said Adam. "I just can't take anymore time for this right now."

Liesl turned her back on him and tugged on my arm. "We can keep looking," she said.

"Feel free," said Adam, turning away. "If you find the gold, just drop me a note."

I looked from Adam to Liesl. I could just hear Pops saying, *Get your chores done before you go off and play. Animals can't wait to be fed.* I figured getting his homework done was for Adam what feeding the animals was for me.

"We'll come back tomorrow," I said. "It's the holiday weekend, right? No school tomorrow. We'll have all day."

"That's right," said Adam, relieved. "If I get my stuff done now then I really will have all day."

"What if those lunks find the gold before we do?" Liesl asked, looking stormy.

"Like I said, you guys can keep going," said Adam.

"We could go tree climbing," I said. Liesl's eyes lit up, and I knew I had hit on the right thing.

But as we came out of the Ingle Building, it was pouring. We stood beneath a fancy, cranberry-colored awning edged in gold.

"I don't have money for a cab," said Adam. "Do you?" Liesl and I both shook our heads.

"We can go back through the tunnel," Liesl said.

"No thanks," said Adam.

I heard someone shouting my name. "Aiden! Aiden!" It was coming from one of the taxis, and then I saw Fernando's head poking out of a window. "Are you wanting a ride?" he shouted over to me.

"We don't have any money!" I shouted back.

"Never mind about that! I owe you a favor for looking after Melo. Come on! I am just waiting for Ana."

We made a run for it, yanked open the backdoor, and slid into the seat. It was so nice and warm and dry in the cab and it had that good smell of cologne and leather. Melo, sitting in the front next to Fernando, squealed happily when he saw us.

After I introduced Adam and Liesl, Fernando wanted to know what we had been doing at the Ingle Building.

"Looking for gold," said Liesl and then clapped her hands over her mouth. "Oops, sorry about that," she mumbled.

"Did you see trolls?" asked Melo, as if nothing out of the ordinary had been said.

I thought of Marisa and Quentin. "Yes," I said. But thinking of trolls reminded me of the story again. "Where does the Bird Lady work?" I asked.

"Outside of town," said Fernando. "I could take you some time. Owls, hawks, falcons—all kinds of birds there. Ah, there she is, Melo, there's your mother." He climbed halfway out of the taxi, yelling and waving, "Ana!"

"*Aie!* What a day!" Ana exclaimed as she flopped into the front seat next to Melo. She let out a huge breath. "The *senhora* is not happy today! She is all out of sorts. I think she is worried about Lady Peregrine and she covers it up by talking on the phone all day long to the bankers, the architects, and goodness knows who else. She wants to build a castle. A castle! Imagine!" Then she seemed to register for the first time that we were there. "Oh, forgive me, I did not see you there! And Melozinho, here you are, I will kiss you now, 3,000 times!" She kissed Melo and then asked him, "What did you do in school today?"

"We learned a song," he said. And he started to sing "Here Comes the Sun." He knew all the words, and his little voice was sweet and perfect.

The three of us in the backseat looked at each other in disbelief. "Zowee," said Liesl when he had finished.

"He's good, *né?*" Fernando asked proudly. "Ana and I think he is very musical but at the moment we cannot pay for music lessons."

"My mom's a music teacher, and she's great teaching little kids," I said, surprising myself. This was a new way of thinking about Mom. "Maybe you could work out something with her."

As Fernando pulled up in front of Adam's apartment house, Adam reached for the door handle and then muttered,

"Thanks. That's the most fun I've had in a long time. I'll see you tomorrow."

Fernando dropped us near an entrance to the park. Even though it was raining, Liesl invited me to come over anyway. We were running along the bike path when she stopped suddenly as we came into the grove of trees.

"There," she said, pointing to two trees that were growing together, "that's my mom and my dad." Her face looked pinched and tight for a moment before she darted off through the rain ahead of me. I stayed there for a moment, thinking at least I had gotten to be with Pops for almost twelve years of my life—Liesl didn't even *remember* her parents.

I bent down and picked up an acorn and, taking aim, threw it as hard as I could toward another oak a few yards away. It landed smack in the center of the trunk with a thud. I felt better, like I could go on without falling apart.

"Wow, that's some arm you've got." A tall boy in a baseball cap came striding up to me. He looked vaguely familiar, but I couldn't place him. "You a ballplayer?"

"Softball," I said.

"Third base," he guessed, as he fell into step with me.

"How'd you know?" I asked.

"I manage a team," he said. "Got an eye for these things."

Liesl was waiting for me at the bottom of the oak tree. The elevator was already coming down. "There you are. Thought you got lost or something," she said to me. Turning to the boy, she asked, "Gareth Pugh, what are you doing here?"

"Willy Wilson and his father are up there," he said, jerking his thumb up to the tree house. "Big powwow going on. I just want to make sure, whatever else happens, Willy doesn't bail on the game that's coming up. Or you, either."

"One-track mind," said Liesl, as she opened the door to the elevator. "Baseball, that's all you think about."

The little living room seemed crowded by the time we stepped into it. Mitch was there and another man and a boy I guessed must be Willy Wilson.

"What's going on?" asked Liesl.

"Meeting," said Mitch. He took a breath and then said, "Mrs. Ingle wants to build a castle in the middle of the grove right here in Gill Park."

17

"This is our cousin, Aiden, and this is Willy Wilson, the owner of Gill Park, and his father, the park's lawyer," said Mitch. "You seem to have met Gareth Pugh, manager of the Gorillas."

The tall man and the two boys nodded. Everyone looked pretty serious. I looked curiously at Willy. When Mom had first mentioned him awhile ago, I hadn't thought much about the fact that he owned the park. The original owner, Otto Pettingill, had willed it to him. Now that I knew the park better, I was amazed a kid my age would be in charge of it.

"How can that old witch even think about doing such a thing?" Liesl asked, throwing herself onto the couch. "She'd have to cut down half the trees."

"Says she'll pay rent for the use of the land," said Mitch, looking somewhat dazed. "It will be a hotel, but she wants it to look like a castle."

"What about *us*?" Liesl asked indignantly. "We're the ones who *live* here."

"Good money," said Willy's father. "Without this deal, you might not get to live here at all." He spoke quietly.

Glancing at Willy again, I noticed he had dark circles under his eyes. He was sitting very still, looking at his feet.

"It's serious, Liesl," Willy's dad went on. "The fund Otto Pettingill set up for the park has taken a big hit. Something has to be done."

Liesl jumped to her feet and went and stood in front of Willy, placing her hands on his shoulders. Her face was pale and the vein above her nose was very blue. "Willy Wilson, are you telling me that you're going to let some old lady cut down our trees and build a dumb *castle* here?"

"Nothing's been decided yet," Willy mumbled. "We only just heard about it today."

"Is it *your* decision, or is it up to all the—*sensible* people?" Liesl asked, jerking her thumb at Willy's father. "Willy Wilson, *you're* the owner, right?"

There was silence in the room for a moment. "He's not quite of age," said Willy's father.

"That's what I figured," said Liesl. She tossed her head and folded her arms tightly against her chest.

"I might not be of age," said Willy slowly. "But I know Mr. Pettingill would have wanted me to make this decision." Willy's father stood up and started pacing around the tiny living room. "I need more time to think, Dad," said Willy. He slumped in his chair, looking miserable.

Willy's father stopped pacing. "We've done a lot of thinking over the past six months about all these issues. We've gone through all the books, looked at all the figures. The only possible glitch is that Mrs. Ingle is counting on paying for this with Gold Falcons. She thinks there is an old collection of them hidden somewhere in the Ingle Building, but she doesn't know where they are yet."

There was a buzzing in my ears, and I felt dizzy. I glanced at Liesl's face. Her eyes were blazing.

Gareth jumped out of his chair and went over and thumped Willy on the arm. "Nothing like playing a little game of baseball to keep you mentally fit. See you at the field tomorrow morning for practice, buddy. You too, Liesl."

"I'd better be going, too," I said, suddenly feeling I needed to get somewhere by myself and think.

Mitch hugged me and told me to come back soon. Willy and his father said good-bye in a distracted sort of way. But Liesl grabbed me hard by the arm and pulled me to one side. "Listen Aiden, we have to find those Gold Falcons before that old dame does. And then we have to *hide* them again so she'll *never* find them." I stared at her. "Don't you see, even if we found them before she does, we wouldn't be allowed to keep 'em."

I nodded numbly, seeing the truth of this. I should have realized a long time ago that I'd never be allowed to keep them. I couldn't imagine why Leo had even encouraged me. As I saw all hope of keeping the farm slipping away, I realized I'd never even told Liesl why I had wanted to find the gold in the first place. She must have thought it was all just for fun. And it was so odd—without the Gold Falcons, I lost my home; *with* them, Liesl lost hers.

As I was going down in the elevator with Gareth Pugh, I knew where I'd seen him. He went to East Park. He was a few years older than me, and he was always playing baseball with a bunch of other kids during free time.

"I go to the same school as you," I said.

"Yeah?" he asked, surprised. He took off his cap and ran his fingers through his hair, which was matted down from wearing the baseball cap. The elevator had reached the ground. "Come out and play ball sometime," he said on his way out.

When I got home, Tony and Merla and Mom were sitting around the living room. I had hardly seen Tony since his bad night at the opera. I knew he was working with all kinds of voice specialists.

"Had a nice day with your friends?" Mom asked.

"Okay," I said. "How's your voice, Tony?" I asked.

Tony shook his head. "Well, just as I suspected, there's nothing wrong with my vocal chords or my throat. I'm afraid it's all in my head. So, I have to figure out what to do about *that*." Tony picked up a page of the newspaper that was spread out all over the floor. "Been looking at the classifieds," he said. "Not much here for an out-of-work opera singer."

I was shocked. "You're not going to be an opera singer anymore?"

"Of course he's going to be an opera singer," said Merla. "But he made an arrangement with his manager. They're going to give him some time off to see if he can solve this problem—"

"But if I don't," said Tony, "I have to figure out what to do next with my life." He jabbed at the newspaper. "Dental hygienist, short-order cook . . ."

"Stop it, Tony!" Merla put a hand on his arm.

The front page was lying faceup. There was a photograph of Mrs. Ingle, and the words CASTLE TO BE BUILT IN GILL PARK IF GOLD FALCONS ARE FOUND in big, bold print.

"Did you hear Mrs. Ingle wants to build a hotel in the Gill Park woods?" I blurted out.

Mom and Merla and Tony all groaned. "It's terrible," said Merla. "We don't want a big building in the middle of the park. I hope she never finds those Gold Falcons."

"But your Mom has some good news," said Tony. "Not everything is dire around here. Tell her, Allegra."

Mom started smiling. "I just came from an audition at a coffeehouse, and our taxi driver, Fernando, was there. When he's not driving, he helps out his cousin who owns the coffeehouse. He said he played some soccer with you today, Aiden, and that you were wonderful to watch his little boy while he played in a game. He also said he picked you and some friends up from the Ingle Building. Well, anyway, they heard me sing, and I've got a gig next Saturday!"

"Oh, that's great, Mom," I said, but I felt a lump in my throat. While hunting for the Falcons, I'd been okay here in Gloria. I hadn't been so homesick. Just as things were beginning to work out for Mom, they were falling apart for me.

"And I made an arrangement with Fernando. Soccer lessons for you, in exchange for music lessons for his little boy. I didn't think you'd mind."

Something in me welled up. "You *never* think I mind."

Mom's expression changed. "Oh Aiden! I was just trying to help you—"

I started shouting, "I just wish you would *ask* me sometimes instead of just *doing* things, like selling the farm. And where's Henrietta?" I looked around and, not seeing her, grabbed her leash and stormed out of the apartment.

I raced across the street to the park and immediately ran into Marisa and Quentin.

"Oh hey, Farmer Girl," said Marisa. She was wearing a yellow raincoat with butterflies all over it and walking a little brown Yorkie that was also wearing a yellow raincoat with butterflies all over it. "Why aren't you out herding the cows?" She and Quentin laughed.

Furious, I walked away, hands balled into fists—and suddenly the park filled up with music. I stopped walking, took a deep breath, and let the music calm me down. It was some kind of classical music, with violins and a flute, and it was soothing. It had stopped raining, and, out of the corner of my eye, I saw something with tiger-striped fur dart through a tangle of bushes.

I felt a rush of relief as Henrietta actually came right up and rubbed against my legs. I squatted down and hugged her tightly, burying my face in her damp fur. She tolerated this for about a half a minute and then wriggled free. But she didn't race off. She trotted with slow, dainty steps just in front of me, ears and tail straight up.

I followed her down a small, narrow path I had never been down before. Pink roses bloomed on either side. We came to a garden surrounded by hedges. It was like a secret little garden, and Ana was bending down, pulling out old tomato plants. I recognized them because we had had a kitchen garden back home. Melo was digging in the dirt with a trowel, singing to himself. Sitting in the corner on a bench was the old woman with all her layers of clothes.

"Kitty," Melo greeted Henrietta with a little cry of joy.

"There's the girl with the cat and the hat!" screeched the old woman.

"Is this your garden?" I asked Ana.

"This is one of my jobs, working for Gill Park," said Ana. "We grow vegetables, help feed people like Old Violet—" She gestured toward the old woman.

"You and Fernando work so hard," I said.

Ana laughed. "Our friends call us the Formigas—*formiga* means ant, *né?* You know the story of the ant and the cicada? The cicada sings all day long while the ant works and works. Sometimes we would like to be more like the cicada, but Fernando and I have a big dream." She leaned closer to me, her face lighting up. "We come to this country to go to school and to work; we learn and we save, and some day we will have enough money to buy a farm. That is our very big dream."

"I help," said Melo, waving his trowel in the air.

"That's true," said Ana proudly. She made a sweeping gesture with her arms. "This is my favorite place, right here. I close my eyes sometimes and pretend it is ours." She brushed her dark hair out of her eyes. "Sometimes our dream seems like a long way off."

"I used to live on a farm," I said. "We just moved here to the city."

"Aiden Farmer who is a farmer," said Ana, smiling. I used to get tired of that joke, but now it made me sad because it wasn't true anymore. "So, we are all like the falcons, *né?* We come from the country to nest in the city. But Aiden, *minha filha*, now that you are here, could I ask you to watch Melo for a moment? I need to go for a rake."

I sat on a bench near Melo. The earth and plant smells were delicious. I could see why Ana liked it so much. But then suddenly I heard voices I knew only too well coming from the other side of the hedge. I could see the bright yellow of a raincoat through the spaces between the leaves.

"I don't know," Marisa was saying. "I still don't have any idea what it means."

Then Quentin said, "ALL WE REALLY HAVE IS TIME." He said it like he was really mad. "I mean, it's such a stupid clue. What does it mean? It sounds like a fortune cookie."

"I've told you a million times, that's the only clue Madame remembers," said Marisa. "That and something about trolls."

"We've looked at every dumb clock in the building, and that's a lot of clocks," said Quentin.

"I still think there's something up with that clock in number 10," said Marisa. "We have to go back there now that grumpy old man isn't there to yell at us. And we need to figure out what the trolls mean."

"That's dumb, too," Quentin said grumpily. "And what's all this for, anyway—so that nut Felix Brown can get his mouse to talk? You don't really believe that's going to happen, do you?"

"Madame believes it, and that's all that matters," said Marisa. With a big, breathy sigh she continued, "She *loves* Felix. She would do anything for him. I think it's sooo romantic."

"Well, I think it's weird, and I'm sick of this so-called treasure hunt."

"Quentin," said Marisa, and I could just imagine her giving him the *Look*. "I think you're forgetting something. The whole point of this is my dance career. And you know what? I have a creepy feeling that Farmer Girl and Nerd Boy are after the gold, too. Every time we turn around, we see them at the building. And we don't want *them* beating us to it, do we?"

By the sound of their voices, I thought they were about to turn the corner and come into the little secret garden. *Don't come in here,* I prayed. They'd know I'd overheard them and then what?

"But why—" Quentin started to say, and I saw his shoe and his leg. But just then the Yorkie started yapping furiously, and Marisa started screaming, "Rudy! Rudy! Come back here! Don't you dare go after that cat!" I checked in a panic for Henrietta, but she was sitting next to Old Violet. I heard them running off, and then it was quiet. And in the next moment, Ana came around the corner with a rake.

"Here we are," said Ana cheerfully. "All's well?"

"Very well," I said. "Melo has been digging happily the whole time."

"He loves to farm, that one," she said.

Black Jack popped through the hedge.

"Jack, you're back!" screeched Old Violet.

Jack's yellow eyes gleamed, and I could have sworn he had a little smile on his face. He leaped up on the bench beside me. "Are you the cat Marisa's dog went after?" I asked him. He rubbed against me, purring. Henrietta came over and jumped up on the bench, too. I slipped the collar around her neck. "I'll let you come back, Henrietta, but it's time to go home now."

But before I left, I asked Ana, "You spend a lot of time

with Mrs. Ingle. Why does she want to build a castle in Gill Park?"

Ana stopped raking and, tilting her head to one side, she said, "Sometimes her mind goes on these little journeys. She is old, *né?* And she misses her daughter, Patsy."

"She called *me* Patsy. She thought I was her *daughter?*"

Ana tilted her head again. "I think it is more that she *wished.* Those two, mother and daughter, had a terrible fight many, many years ago. Now Mrs. Ingle thinks if she builds a castle and calls it Patsy's Castle, Patsy will hear about it and come home." She laughed a little musical laugh. "When she was a little girl, all Patsy wanted to be was a princess and live in a castle."

Like the girl in the treasure hunt story, I thought. I stopped for a moment, a little startled by that discovery. "Where *is* Patsy?" I asked.

Ana shook her head and lifted her shoulders. "Across the sea," she said. "She lives in England, but no one knows where."

I left Ana and Melo and Old Violet and started walking Henrietta home. On the way I called Adam. I told him all about Mrs. Ingle and the Gold Falcons and Patsy's Castle. I told him how Liesl said now we really *had* to find the Falcons and then hide them. Then I told him about the conversation between Marisa and Quentin and the clue I had overheard.

"Wait a minute!" Adam said. "Maybe Mr. Ingle and Mr. Balboni set up the hunt together, but the FLY TO E15 clue is in your hat, Aiden. Think about it. It's a *Balboni* hat. I bet that collection of Gold Falcons belonged to your great-grandfather."

I didn't say anything for a moment as I took this in.

"And look, we're on a roll. We're so close. We just have

to head over to the west wing tomorrow, and, who knows, maybe we're done. Marisa and Quentin don't have a chance with their one dumb clue, and Mrs. Ingle doesn't know *anything* or she would have already found the gold a hundred years ago."

"Adam," I said, "maybe you *will* go to Harvard some day."

When I got off the phone, someone was playing the bouncy harmonica music into the park again. I bounced all the way home, and when I came into the apartment I gave Mom a hug. She was smart enough not to say anything.

The next morning I carried Henrietta across the street and let her go in the park. "You can go free," I said, "but stay away from the cars." And then I went to Leo's.

"So," he said. "How's it going?"

I made a face. "We were finding the clues just fine and I even met someone who knows the story, but—"

"Wait a minute, wait a minute," said Leo. He came around from behind the counter. "Who knows the story?"

"The Bird Lady," I said. Leo looked at me blankly. "She fixes up injured birds. I met her at a soccer game where I was taking care of a little kid who was having a hard time. She came up and calmed him down with a story about a girl who goes looking for gold because she wants to build a castle, and there are trolls and all these funny, random numbers that turned out to be apartment numbers."

Leo's mouth dropped open. "What did she look like?" he asked, sounding a little hoarse.

"She was on the older side," I said. "Long, white hair—I don't know, nice-looking. You must know her if she knows the story, right? Who is she?"

Leo made a sort of strangled sound in his throat. "I'm not sure," he said. "I don't know if it's possible—"

"I want to find her and have her finish the story," I said. "She disappeared before the end of it. But Leo, there's kind of a problem. Now Mrs. Ingle wants to find the Gold Falcons so she can build a castle in the grove in Gill Park."

Leo nodded. "I read about that."

"Did you know she wants to call it Patsy's Castle?"

Leo groaned. "To lure her back home," he said. And I went on to tell him about how Liesl wanted us to find the Gold Falcons so we could hide them again to prevent Mrs. Ingle from building in the grove. Leo groaned again. "But my friend Adam thinks they might be Balboni Falcons," I said. "Do you think they are?"

Leo looked startled. "I never thought of that. Maybe they are," he said slowly. "Maybe they are."

My mind was swirling as I walked through the park to meet Adam at the bottom of Liesl's tree. He was there waiting for me. I opened the gray box on the tree trunk and buzzed for Liesl.

"What's up?" a crackly voice came through the speaker.

"It's us," I said.

"Be down in a jiffy," said Liesl.

As the elevator started shimmying down to the ground, Adam said, "Someday I really would like to go up there."

"Be nicer to Liesl and maybe she'll invite you," I said.

Adam grunted.

Liesl rolled her eyes when Adam told her his theory about the Balboni Falcons. "I don't believe it," she said. "And come on, Adam, how are we going to know when we find them if they are Ingle or Balboni Falcons?"

"Maybe there is a certificate of ownership," said Adam.

"And if there isn't, then we follow your plan, Liesl—we make it *impossible* for anyone else to find them. At least Marisa and Quentin won't ever get them."

"Yeah!" said Liesl. That didn't seem like such a victory to me, not compared to how it would feel to be able to keep the farm. "How are we going today?" she asked. "Under or over?"

"We could just walk there," said Adam. "It's not raining or anything."

"West wing, here we come," said Liesl happily.

Someone was playing Spanish guitar music into the park. Liesl clapped and stamped and danced her way along the bike path, and Adam tried to look as if he didn't know her.

As we came into the lobby, we saw signs for a swimming pool, a ballroom, an auditorium, and the concert hall. "This place has everything," said Adam.

"But she needs *more*," said Liesl. "She has to have a castle in *my* woods. Hang on," she said, stopping suddenly, "do you see what I see?"

A couple of people were walking around the lobby with weird-looking gizmos.

"Metal detectors," said Adam. "I don't believe this. Mrs. Ingle must have set them up."

"It's so *unfair*," said Liesl, looking stormy. "Come on!"

We ran to the hallway where the bank of elevators looked exactly like the one in the east wing.

"Let's go up in number 20 where Ernie is now," I said.

As the elevator arrived and the doors opened, we were amazed to find Rosie, not Ernie, at the controls. "Rosie!" said a woman who had been in the hallway waiting with us. "There you are! I've been looking everywhere for you."

"Ernie had some things to do, and I'm on my break, so I'm taking his shift," said Rosie. "What do you need, Adele?"

"Dorota wanted me to tell you we're all going to Debby's spelling bee tonight—we're meeting for supper at her house, six o'clock tonight."

"All right, dolling, thanks for letting me know, and here is my new gang of children—it's like the old days, isn't it, Adele, having these children here. Come on in, dollings, and where are you off to today?"

"Eleventh floor, please," I said as we stepped in.

"Listen, my dollings, you *are* looking for Gold Falcons, am I right?"

"Yes, Rosie," I said. "Can you help us? Do you remember anything about the old treasure hunt?"

Rosie shook her head. "I'm telling you honestly if I had the faintest idea I'd have looked for those Falcons myself. All I remember was there was a story about a mountaintop that shone like gold in the sun. That part always stuck in my mind. But I just wanted to tell you, don't let Grip catch you at this—he doesn't like kids running around the place."

We rode up the rest of the way looking at the photographs that were plastered all over the walls. Rosie proudly pointed out who was who—the big, glossy black and white was of Rosie and Ernie twenty years ago. A woman who looked like a younger Rosie was Lizzie, their daughter. There was a wonderful picture of Leo, taken a long time ago when he still had black hair, and there was a nice-looking young couple, Minnie and her husband. And then there were about a hundred other pictures of all the uncles and aunts and cousins and nephews and nieces and grandchildren and great-grandchildren. I wished there was one of Patsy. I wanted to see if we did look alike.

"Here we are," said Rosie, "11th floor."

"Thanks, Rosie, be back soon."

"Trolls!" she suddenly exclaimed on our way out. "There were a lot of trolls!"

I sighed. "Everyone remembers the trolls."

We ran down the hall until we found apartment number 1,114. The excitement of the hunt came rushing back, and we immediately flung ourselves down on the floor, inspecting the bottom of the door. "It's there, it's there," Liesl screeched. It *was* there—the cartoon bird with its funny, floppy wings. It had a big fat number 12 on its belly.

"It's smack in the middle," said Adam. "So that means the next clue is in the middle part of the Ingle Building, 12th floor."

"Let's go!" said Liesl excitedly.

As we ran back down the hall to Rosie's elevator, I wondered *where* on the 12th floor we were supposed to go.

Felix Brown was in Rosie's elevator when it arrived. He was wearing a different sweatshirt today. It said MICE ARE NICE on the front. "Miss Balboni, I was thinking about you last night," he said.

"Farmer," I said. "I'm Aiden *Farmer*."

Felix didn't seem to hear me. "Your mother is Allegra Balboni, I believe, isn't that right?" As I nodded, he said, "She had a lovely voice, but I understand she ran off with a farmer—"

"That was my pops," I said. "Herb Farmer."

"Ah," he said, "Herb Farmer was a farmer, ha ha. Well, the young Ingle boy, Bertie, ran off to be a farmer, too, you know."

"I didn't know that," I said.

"Oh yes, so many stories to be told, but I tell you what, I'm on my way up to the rooftop café. Why don't you and your young friends join me for a snack. My treat." Nose and whiskers poked out of the neckband of Felix's sweatshirt. "And Charles would enjoy your company, too, I'm sure."

Adam and Liesl gave me a slightly panicky look, but it seemed impossible to say no. As we came out on to the rooftop, Liesl muttered, "Don't look now, but Marisa and Quentin are up here."

"Ah," said Felix, spotting them. "More of your young friends. Come along, you two," he said to Marisa and Quentin, "and join us. I do so enjoy telling young people about the old days."

A lot of panicky looks were being exchanged now, between Marisa and Quentin, between the three of us, but Felix somehow managed to tow us all through the door to the café and was signaling to a waiter. We found ourselves being led to a table with a white tablecloth and a flower arrangement in the middle.

"Miss Balboni," Felix said to me. "Do us the honor." He pulled out a chair next to his. "Charles will like that." As we all sat down, Felix extracted Charles from his sweatshirt and placed him on the table. Marisa sort of gasped and shuddered, but Quentin said, "Cool." I sat with my hat in my lap, remembering Mom's constant nagging about not wearing hats in restaurants. "Treat coming soon, Charles," said Felix. "Just hold on."

A busboy came over and poured water, and then the waiter appeared.

"Peppermint-stick ice cream for everyone. With chocolate sauce," said Felix.

"I'm-um-uh lactose intolerant." Adam tugged on his hair, looking uncomfortable.

"I—don't like peppermint-stick," said Quentin.

"I don't eat chocolate," said Marisa.

Felix frowned. "Nonsense!" he exclaimed. "Kids who won't eat peppermint-stick ice cream with chocolate sauce! What is the world coming to? That will be seven dishes of peppermint-stick ice cream with chocolate sauce," he said to the waiter. "Peppermint-stick with chocolate sauce is Charles's favorite."

An awkward silence settled around the table. Marisa was giving me the *Look,* as if it were my fault we were trapped sitting here with each other. I cleared my throat nervously. "Um, Bertie Ingle," I said. "Why did he run off to be a farmer?"

"Well, it's like this," said Felix. "I'll start at the beginning, if you don't mind." Everyone did mind, because everyone shifted uncomfortably in their chairs. "When I was a young boy living here in the Ingle Building, Edward Ingle, the grandson of James Ingle, the man who built this building, was a handsome, cultured, brilliant businessman. One day he married a woman, quite a bit younger than he, named Felicity, and she was beautiful and glamorous and elegant and fun and full of life." Felix sighed deeply, his face glowing at the memory. "If you could have seen it—it was like a fairy tale come to life around here in those days—grand parties in the ballroom—men in tails, women in diamonds and fur coats."

Charles, sitting on the tablecloth between Felix and me, squeaked slightly.

"Yes, Charles," said Felix, "sorry to say, fur coats *were*

popular back then. Well, in any case, as children growing up in this building, we loved nothing better than stealing down the stairs at night to watch the goings-on. I believe, Miss Balboni," he said, turning to me, "it was the heyday of your great-grandfather's career. Grand concerts! Ballet companies from Russia!" He pointed at Marisa. "And yes, young lady, it is when your friend, Nan Peters, I beg your pardon, Madame Petrovna, first fell in love with ballet. And opera!" Felix pointed a finger at me. "You want to talk about opera! The Opera Hall was packed every night. Singers from all over the world."

The waiter appeared with the ice cream. Charles plunged right into his, lapping away. Liesl and I picked up our spoons and dug in. Adam, Marisa, and Quentin sat glumly looking down at theirs.

"The Ingle children were born during that glorious time," Felix went on. "First Patsy and then four years later Bertie—and, oh Charles, you're getting chocolate on your whiskers." Felix took his napkin and dabbed at Charles's face. "Patsy grew up to be a feisty, independent girl, and young Bertie—he was a lively one, too. Great favorite with all of us. He loved those treasure hunts Mr. Balboni and Mr. Ingle thought up to entertain the children. I was a bit too old for them myself."

We all leaned toward Felix at the mention of the treasure hunts.

"But then, one day—oh dear." Felix paused. "Mr. Ingle contracted the influenza."

"That's the flu," Adam said, as if we might not know.

"Oh thanks for telling us, Adam," said Quentin sarcastically.

Felix nodded. "Yes," he said with a deep sigh. "The flu.

He was ill for several weeks and then there followed a terrible time."

Felix stopped speaking for a moment. Charles, who seemed to have become tired of his ice cream, was now wandering across the table making chocolate footprints on the white tablecloth. He was heading toward my dish. I fluffed up my napkin and put it on the table to make a barrier.

"It was a terrible time," said Felix again. "No more fancy balls. No more evenings out at the opera. No more treasure hunts. Felicity Ingle threw herself into her husband's business. She worked all the time and had not a moment to spare for her own children. The great family of elevator operators in this building became family to Patsy and Bertie, Rosie and Ernie especially, because their two children, Leo and Lizzie, were best of friends with the Ingle children."

Adam was tufting his hair, and Liesl was licking chocolate off her spoon. Marisa was folding and unfolding her napkin. Quentin was staring into his cell phone, which he held in his lap. Charles was nibbling the flowers in the center of the table.

"They spent hours together, those children, riding up and down the elevators, doing their homework together, playing games. It was Rosie they'd confide their troubles to and Ernie who helped with school projects. And Mrs. Ingle, she paid not a bit of attention to those kids. Until—" and here Felix lowered his voice dramatically, "Patsy fell in love with Leo Schwartz."

We all sat up again.

Felix jabbed the tablecloth with a finger. "Well then, you better believe Mrs. Ingle had a royal *fit*. She forbade Patsy from ever seeing Leo again."

Poor Leo, I thought, and Marisa, gazing dreamily into

space, said, "It sounds like Romeo and Juliet. Did Patsy drink vile poison and die?"

Felix looked a bit flustered. "Patsy did not—no—she did not do anything as dramatic as that; she was sent away to Europe, to some sort of finishing school, and that was the end of their romance. Very sad, really. Poor Leo never married. And Patsy never married, either, as far as I know, but after that she never really had much to do with her mother or the Ingle Building ever again."

We sat without saying anything for a moment, taking this in. Poor Leo, I thought again. If there *was* any chance the castle in the park could bring Patsy back, well, wouldn't that be a good thing?

"And Bertie?" I asked.

"Ah now, finally, we get to Bertie," said Felix. "I believe the boy was very upset about the whole Leo and Patsy situation, but Mrs. Ingle sent him away—to one of those progressive schools where kids work on a farm, where you get up early to milk the cows before you have your lessons. And he liked the life. He could have lived here in the lap of luxury, but no, when he grew up, he chose to be a farmer."

"There's nothing wrong with being a farmer," I said.

"Mooooo," said Quentin, and then stopped abruptly and said, "Ow." Liesl was sitting beside him, smiling like a demon.

"Bertie sent home letters to Rosie and Ernie for a while," Felix went on. "But fewer and fewer as time went on and then we lost all trace of him."

Marisa suddenly scraped back her chair and stood up and said, "Well, we must be going now, thank you for the ice cream. Come on, Quentin, we have to go."

"Well!" said Felix standing up. "My pleasure, I—" But

Marisa and Quentin rushed off before he could say another word. "Oh dear, I hope I wasn't too boring. But in any case, I need to be getting back to work myself. Now, where is Charles?" He began to look around frantically. "He was just here, where has he gone?" Liesl, Adam, and I helped him look. We checked the flowers and under the tablecloth and down on the floor under the chairs. "Charles, where are you? Oh my, this is terrible!"

The waiter came over, looking concerned. "I've lost my mouse," Felix said to him. "And I have to find him—I'm just so close, especially now with the possibility of finding gold—"

At the mention of gold, Liesl pulled me by the arm. "Come on, let's go. We can't waste another minute."

"I hope you find Charles," I said, "and thank you very much for the ice cream."

Felix seemed not to hear us as we ran out of the café.

"Hello, dollings," said Rosie as we stepped back into her elevator. "Now where are you going?"

"We have to get to the middle of the Ingle Building," said Adam. "So down."

"Wait," I said, realizing I'd left my hat. "I have to go back up. My hat—"

"Get it later," said Adam.

"I can go back up, dolling," said Rosie.

"Later," said Liesl.

"Okay, okay," I said.

I stared at the photograph of Leo when he was young. I couldn't help blurting out, "Rosie, how come you and Ernie stayed working here after Mrs. Ingle said Leo couldn't marry Patsy?" Then I was embarrassed. "I'm sorry—Felix Brown told us—"

But Rosie didn't seem offended. "I've asked myself that same question a thousand times, dolling, but I have to say it was out of loyalty to the Ingle Building itself. When Mr. Ingle became very ill, he called us into his room and said, 'You'll look out for the Ingle Building, won't you, Rosie and Ernie? Please help my wife to keep it going.'"

As the doors to the elevator opened at the bottom, we all jumped as Grip strode into the elevator. "Someone reported kids as having stolen private property," he said, glowering at Adam, Liesl, and me.

"If you're referrin' to these kids, they haven't stolen anything," said Rosie, looking disgusted.

Grip yanked at the brim of his cap. "I got a call from the west wing café," he said. "Felix Brown reported missing his prize show mouse. I went up there, and we looked everywhere. Then Felix tells me he treats a bunch of kids to ice cream. So I think to myself, ha, kids, they took advantage of him. They walked off with his prize mouse, that's what they did. So let's just check your pockets."

"We didn't steal his mouse," said Adam indignantly, but he turned his pockets inside out and showed Grip his wallet and cell phone. Liesl pulled out a handful of chalk. I stuck my hands into the pockets of my jacket and . . . my hand struck fur.

"Charles! What are you doing here?" I scooped him out. His whole body, slightly sticky and smelling of chocolate, was trembling as he gazed at me.

"Did I tell you or not tell you?" Grip demanded.

"I did not steal this mouse!" I said. "He must have jumped into my pocket when I wasn't looking."

"Yeah, yeah," said Grip, "just hand him over and I won't press charges."

But Charles had his own ideas. He leaped out of my hands and landed on the floor. Grip lunged for him, but Charles was too quick and scrabbled into the corner of the elevator behind Rosie's stool where she had her knitting bag and several other bags.

"Come out of there, mouse!" Grip crouched down, searching around in the bags, and then he yelped, straightening up quickly and shaking his hand. "It bit me!" he yelled. "That blasted rodent bit me!"

"It was just a little nip. He didn't even break the skin," said Rosie scornfully. "You're scaring him with all that yelling. Let him be. I'll make sure he doesn't escape, and then I'll return him to Felix."

"That mouse is supposed to be worth millions," said Grip. He scowled at us. "And you kids, I should call security on you, but seeing as how we got the mouse back, just get out of here and don't let me see you on these premises again."

Rosie stood up, her hands on her hips. "They happen to be *my* friends."

"Either they move on or I call security." Grip yanked on his cap again and, continuing to fume, marched off.

"Charles must have crept into my pocket. I didn't take him, Rosie," I said, bending down to pick up Rosie's knitting. I poked around her bags, but Charles was nowhere to be seen.

"I don't believe that Felix guy," Adam said grumpily. "First he talks our heads off, and then he accuses us of stealing his dumb mouse!"

"Felix is a little over the top about that mouse," said Rosie, "and Grip likes nothing better than to stir up trouble between folks. From what I hear, he's put some sorry little excuse for an operator into Ernie's old elevator. Love to be a fly on the wall and see how Mrs. Ingle takes to her."

"That's just where we're going now," I said. "We can check her out."

"Oh, splendid! Can't wait to hear what you think of her. Ta ta, dollings, and keep those eyes peeled for gold."

21

The doors to number 10 opened, and the operator sitting at the controls looked like she was only a few years older than I was. She was slouched on her stool in the corner, busy texting on her cell phone. "Where ya goin'?" she asked, without looking up.

"Twelfth floor, please," I said as we stepped in.

"Oh yeah?" She peered at us suspiciously. "D'ya live there? Never seen ya here before."

"My uncle lives there," said Liesl without batting an eyelash.

"Yeah? Who's your uncle?"

"He's a hermit—he never leaves his apartment—hasn't left it for fifty years," said Adam.

The operator raised her eyebrows. "I never heard of a hermit living here."

"No, well, you wouldn't, because he's a hermit," said Liesl.

We reached the 12th floor, and the operator stared at us curiously as we ran out of the elevator. As soon as the doors closed, Adam and Liesl high-fived each other. "Nice work," he said. I realized the two of them were beginning to get along.

"We're here on the 12th floor, but where do we go?" asked Liesl.

Adam and Liesl looked at me expectantly. My heart sank.

"Go on. Close your eyes, talk to Mr. Ingle," said Adam.

I closed my eyes. I tried to remember the story as the Bird Lady had told it. Were there other clues besides numbers? I opened my eyes. "Sorry, he's not talking today."

"You're kidding!" said Liesl.

Worried, I plunged my hands into my pockets. And found Charles. "Good grief! Charles must have crept back into my pocket again, maybe when I was picking up Rosie's knitting."

"Charles led us to that first clue," said Liesl. "Maybe he'll lead us to this one."

"Why not?" said Adam, making a face. "Follow the magic mouse."

I brought Charles out of my pocket and set him gently on the floor. "Find the clue, Charles," I said. Nose and whiskers quivering, Charles blinked a few times. Then he took off, zigzagging across the hall from door to door.

The dark hall widened suddenly and brightened. The walls turned into windows, and the ceiling had big, glass skylights. The hall still ran through the middle, but we were surrounded on both sides by an indoor garden. Charles disappeared into a clump of geranium-looking things. "Yikes, Charles, get out of there," I said.

Charles was sniffing at the base of a block of granite that was plunked in the middle of the garden. "This is a clock," said Adam, now standing in the plants himself. Bronze numbers were arranged on the top in a circle like a clock with a bronze falcon in the middle. The falcon was a miniature of the one on the Ingle Building mountain—same pose with its wings outspread. *"All that we really,"* he said, reading words chiseled into the sides as he walked around it, *"have is . . .*

". . . *time,"* I said, feeling prickles up my neck.

"How'd you *know*?" he asked.

"Remember, it's the clue Madame Petrovna gave Marisa."

"Ack," said Adam.

Charles scrabbled out of the geraniums. I leaned down and picked him up. "Good work, Charles, now just tell us what it means." I patted his head and put him back in my pocket.

"ALL THAT WE REALLY HAVE IS TIME?" Liesl repeated. "What *does* it mean?"

I shook my head. I pulled the watch out of my pocket and stared at it as if it had some secret about time it wasn't telling me. "So we're stuck in this hunt in the same place as Marisa and Quentin."

We walked slowly down the hall to wait for the elevator. When it arrived, it was carrying not only the dopey operator, but Ana, who beamed when she saw us. "Oh my, it always makes my heart glad to see you kids. I'm telling you, things are not so easy upstairs," she added, brushing the hair out of her face.

"Going down," the operator said in a bored tone of voice without looking up from her cell phone.

The three of us crowded toward the back of the elevator where the clock was. "ALL THAT WE REALLY HAVE IS TIME," I said. I put my hand on it, wondering, like Marisa and Quentin, if it had anything to do with the hunt.

"Get off the clock," said the operator without looking up. "The old lady told me to keep people off the clock."

Ana made a face and stepping toward the girl she said, "Excuse me one minute."

The girl looked up. "Yeah?"

"Mrs. Een-go-lee would not like to be referred to as 'the old lady,' and she would not like to see you with your phone."

"And who are you? The queen of England?" the elevator operator said, sneering at Ana.

"I know what Mrs. Een-go-lee likes and does not like," said Ana, her dark eyes snapping.

The girl sucked in her cheeks. "It's so stupid," she said. "What am I supposed to do with myself in here all day long?" But she put the phone away.

Turning to us, Ana said, "Fernando will be here to pick me up. I know he will not mind giving you a lift again."

Adam was staring at the grandfather clock. "I wonder how this clock even works in here—I mean you'd think the motion of going up and down would affect the movement of the pendulum."

I remembered how Pops had asked the same question.

"Ernie could tell you," I said.

"Too bad Ernie isn't here," said Adam loudly.

Stone-faced, the girl looked straight ahead of her.

There was an awkward silence as the doors opened. "Bye-bye," Ana sang out cheerfully as we left the elevator. "That girl will not last more than one minute with Mrs. Een-go-lee," she added as the doors closed behind us.

As we went outside and stood waiting for Fernando, I suddenly remembered my hat. "I'll be right back," I said.

I raced back into the building and ran as fast as I could down the hallway over to the west wing. There was a sign on elevator number 20 saying CLOSED. Going up in number 19, the operator was a friendly old guy. "Are you one of Rosie's brothers?" I asked him.

He nodded. "Stefan," he said.

"Oh! I've heard about you!" I exclaimed.

"You *have*?" Stefan looked pleased. "You've heard of *me*?"

The café was just closing as I rushed in the door. I went over to the waiter who had served us. "Did you see a hat—I was sitting at that table over there with the mouse—and I left my hat." The waiter rubbed his chin.

"You're the one who stole the mouse?"

"I didn't steal the mouse," I said indignantly. "It was an old-fashioned sort of wool cap. Have you seen it?"

"Maybe the mouse stole the hat?" the waiter joked, but then he asked the manager, the other waiters, and the busboy. No one remembered seeing the hat. They told me to check back in a day or two. Maybe it would show up.

It was an awful feeling, losing my hat.

The others were already in Fernando's cab when I walked out of the Ingle Building. "They didn't have it," I said, as I slid into the backseat next to Liesl and Adam.

22

Leo called me when I got home. "Find anything today?" he asked.

I told him about the clock in the indoor garden that said, "ALL THAT WE REALLY HAVE IS TIME." It's the same clue Madame Petrovna gave Marisa and Quentin."

"Ah, it came from that clock, of course, the one with the little bronze falcon," said Leo.

"All the clues have to do with birds or time," I said.

"Yes," said Leo, "although I'm not sure how that helps."

"But Charles led us there—it must be important," I said.

"Charles?" he asked.

"It's a long story," I said. And then I thought, Good grief! Charles! I looked around frantically for him. Where had he gotten to?

In the middle of the night there was a crash.

I sat up in my bed, clutching the railing as I heard another crash.

"What in the world?" Tony was up and out of his bedroom. He turned on a light.

"It's Henrietta," said Mom sleepily. "She's chasing something."

A second later Henrietta leaped up on my bed. Something in her mouth dropped out and ran across the covers toward me. In another second, I felt a mouse tail whip across my face. My heart sank. I had been rudely awakened plenty of times in my farm bedroom with exactly that same sensation. Henrietta was using my bed as hunting territory.

"Henrietta's chasing a mouse," I said sleepily.

"Great," said Uncle Tony with a groan.

The mouse stopped between me and Henrietta. It was large and white with dark eyes patches and dark ears and a bottom third that looked like it had been dipped in black paint. Good grief! I was fully awake now.

"Charles?" I asked. His big, bright eyes looked terrified.

"Who is Charles?" Tony asked grumpily.

Charles ran up my arm, his little feet scratchy against my skin, and onto my shoulder. His whiskers tickled my neck.

"He's Felix Brown's mouse," I said. "He's, um, a special mouse. Best-in-show . . . and . . ."

Henrietta, at the end of my bed, swished her tail back and forth and growled a rumbly, low growl. Charles tumbled off my shoulder and onto the covers beside me and lay on his back with his eyes shut, his mouth open, his feet sticking straight up in the air.

Henrietta blinked, trying to figure out what was going on. I managed to lean forward and push her off the bed. She landed with a thump below me.

"Egad, it's raining cats," Tony exclaimed.

"Charles, the cat is off the bed now. You can sit up," I said.

"Are you *talking* to that mouse, Aiden?" Mom asked.

Charles righted himself with a flip. "I knew it," I said. "I knew you were faking it."

"Aiden! You *are* talking to that mouse!"

"He understands me," I said. "Felix Brown, his owner, has been working on zapping the part of his brain that controls language—"

"I'm trying to control *my* language," said Tony. His face appeared at the edge of my bed. Charles's little head snapped up, and he stared at Tony.

"I think he must have jumped into my jacket pocket so he could meet you! He loves opera, and he loves you, Tony."

"Oh good grief, Aiden."

Henrietta was up on the bureau again, her tail swishing as she prepared to leap up again. Something got knocked off the bureau.

"Do you think we could put the mouse—Charles—whatever his name is—away somewhere safe for the night so we could get some sleep?" Mom asked.

"Come on, Charles." Tony scooped him up, holding him in the cupped palm of one hand. "Maybe you'd like to spend the night in the bread box."

"I bet he's hungry and thirsty, too, Tony," I said. "You'd better feed him. And then maybe you could sing him a lullaby."

The next morning I made a little nest for Charles out of a box, putting some ripped newspaper in it and poking holes in the top. "You're coming to school with me today," I said to him as I put on my blazer. "You can sit in my pocket some of the time, but you have to stay out of sight because mice probably aren't allowed at the East Park Day School. Do you understand?" Charles blinked his eyes and twitched his whiskers. "And after school, I'll take you back to Felix."

I didn't have a chance to see how he felt about this because at that moment Henrietta chose to jump from the bed onto the bookcase. Charles dove into my pocket.

It was fun being at school with Charles. As I stood in the hallway in the seventh grade cubby area just outside our homeroom, I didn't care so much that all the girls, as usual, grouped around Marisa and completely ignored me. But then to my surprise, Marisa waved and said, "Hi Aiden." I looked at her suspiciously. Asha, trailing behind her, looked just as startled as I felt. Marisa broke away from the other girls and said, "Have I told you I love your hair, Aiden? Blondes have more fun, right? I want to dye my hair, but my mom won't let me."

I looked at Marisa closely. She must have figured out we were looking for the Falcons, and she was trying to find out what I knew.

Keeping one hand lightly curled around Charles, I went into our homeroom.

"Aiden!" Adam came right over to me. I was glad I had a friend at school now.

"Guess who showed up at our apartment last night?" I said, pointing to my pocket.

Adam peered in and raised his eyebrows. "Holy mouse tails," he said.

Marisa waltzed into the room and came right up to Adam and said, "Hey Adam, how's it going?"

Adam's jaw dropped and he closed his eyes and put a hand up to his heart and started gasping and moaning. A group of kids gathered around him. Mr. Jenkins, who had been busy at his desk, strode over. "What's going on? Adam, are you hurt?"

Adam opened his eyes. "My heart—" he said, clutching his chest. "I think it stopped—Marisa actually said hello to me."

Everyone started groaning, The bell rang and classes started, but there was a different feeling in the homeroom, as if some tension had been removed. It had something to do with Marisa. She wasn't turning and sneering at people or raising one eyebrow in that way she had. I tested it out, asking her if I could borrow a pencil, and she said, "Of course." Normally, Marisa would have rolled her eyes and said something like, "Don't they have pencils on *farms*, Farmer Girl?"

At recess, she surprised me again. "Let's play some ball," she said. I didn't remember Marisa ever playing baseball before. She marched straight out onto the field and said to Gareth Pugh, "We're playing." She scooped up two gloves that were in an equipment box beside the field and threw one to me.

"Hang on tight," I said to Charles. "If I have to run, you're going to get jounced around."

Recess was twenty minutes long. In that twenty minutes, I managed to catch a pop-up and, when my team went to bat, I hit a single and got to first. Morgan and Chad high-fived me as the end-of-recess bell rang. "Didn't know you could play so good," they said.

"Nice going," said Gareth. "Come out and play more often."

At lunch, first Adam came over to sit with me, then Morgan and then Chad. Then Marisa. "Mind if I sit here?" she asked.

"I guess it's okay," I said. That meant Asha, too, and a swarm of other girls.

Adam clutched his chest again. "I can't handle being popular," he said.

"Be quiet, Adam," I said.

Throughout the day, I'd been giving Charles little breaks

by putting him in the box with some bits of bread and water. After lunch, back in the classroom, I took him out of my pocket and put him in the box with some food I'd taken from the lunchroom. "What is that, Aiden?" Chad asked, coming over to me.

"It's a mouse," I said in a low voice, "but don't tell anyone." I realized with a thrill that he hadn't called me Farmer Girl.

Chad whistled. "Whoa, that's cool."

The bell rang, and the kids settled down for the class after lunch. I actually raised my hand a few times.

Mr. Jenkins finally called on me. "Yes, Farmer Girl?"

My heart was bumping away a mile a minute. I said, "My name is NOT Farmer Girl."

All the kids' heads whipped around to look at me.

"When people call me that, it puts me in a really bad mooooood, Mr. Jenkins."

Someone giggled.

Mr. Jenkins cleared his throat. "Ah, what was the answer to the question, Aiden?"

Charles chose that exact moment to leap out of my pocket and onto the desk. Asha, who was sitting beside me, started to scream. Everyone else started either screaming or yelling.

Yikes. It's just a *mouse*, I wanted to say, and a tame one at that.

Charles was freaked out. He stood up on his backs legs for a moment, ears back, eyes bulging in his head, and then took a flying leap off the desk. He skittered behind a pile of books that were on the floor next to Morgan, and, as Morgan reached down to grab him, he ran frantically for the grand-father clock, disappearing underneath it.

There was an ominous silence in the classroom.

"Aiden Farmer," said Mr. Jenkins. "Whatever possessed you to bring a mouse to school?"

A million answers flickered through my mind, some of them rude like Charles is a smart mouse and probably would get a whole lot out of going to school, but all I said was, "I'm sorry, Mr. Jenkins. I won't do it again."

"No you won't, and furthermore, you'll miss sports this afternoon and not leave this classroom until you've collected that mouse."

"I'll stay and help her," said Adam.

"Very kind of you, I'm sure," said Mr. Jenkins, and I breathed more easily, seeing that I wasn't going to get into trouble.

When the bell for sports rang, everyone left the classroom. I went over to the clock and lay down in front of it on my stomach. "Charles," I said, "it's safe now, you can come out."

There was a scritching sound, maybe of toenails, and Charles suddenly appeared inside the glass case. He jumped onto the big, round brass disk of the pendulum. He swung back and forth for a few seconds and then, climbing up the rod it was suspended from, disappeared behind the clock face.

"Oh great," said Adam.

"On our clock at home there's a side door at the top— yep, this one has it, too." I opened the little door, and there was Charles's tail. "You could hide a bunch of Gold Falcons in a place like that!"

Adam slapped a hand against his forehead. "Hang on," he said, "I have sort of an idea." He went over to the chalkboard. "Can you remember the sequence of floors we've been to on the treasure hunt? I mean the numbers we were sent to? It started with 15, right?"

"It was 15-3-11-12," I said, slowly naming each one.

Adam wrote those numbers on the board. Then he started started writing the alphabet in large capital letters, starting with *A*. Under *A*, he put 1, under *B*, he put 2, and so on, ending with a 15 under the letter *L*. Then he circled the number 15 with its matching letter, *O*, and then the number 3 with its matching letter *C* until he spelled out O-C-K-L.

"See?" he said, his face flushed.

"Ockle?"

"No," said Adam cheerfully. "You have to unscramble the letters. *C-L-O-K*. It's *clock* without the second *C*."

"Oh my gosh! Adam, you're a genius!"

"Charles is the genius," said Adam. "I was sort of playing around with the numbers in my head last night, but when I saw him just now in the clock it just fell into place. And think about it—what's in elevator number 10? And what is that clue? ALL THAT WE REALLY HAVE IS TIME. It might even be the reason that clock is in there. I mean, an elevator is a funny place for a grandfather clock."

Charles's nose and whiskers appeared out of the little door.

"Charles, come on out now," I said. "The coast is clear. Hey, Adam, let's go back to the Ingle Building right now. We've missed most of sports anyhow." Then I stopped, looking at Adam. "Oh no, you can't. You have HAH."

"I can miss HAH for once."

I pressed my hand against my heart. "Oh my poor heart, I can't believe what I'm hearing."

"You have to have priorities in life," said Adam, gathering his stuff together.

"We should stop by Liesl's school and get her," I said. "But first we've got to get Charles." But Charles had already run down the clock and was scampering up the leg of my desk. "Been quite a day for you, Charles," I said, scooping him into my pocket. "Hope you've enjoyed it."

23

"The Gill Park Gallery School isn't that far from here," said Adam. "Wait till you see it."

It wasn't long before we were standing in front of a tall building with flowers and leaves and animals all over the front of it. We went up the front steps and through the door into the lobby. There were carousels with postcards of paintings and tables with art books on them. It looked like a museum store.

"This is a *school*? It's even weirder than East Park," I said.

"You see," said Adam.

A woman with spiky red hair and neon green eyes sat behind a counter. The cost of going into the gallery was posted above her. "May I help you?" she asked.

"We're looking for Liesl Summer," I said.

"She'll be in the main classroom—just head up the stairs, you'll find it."

We walked across a marble floor, passing marble statues and marble columns.

We kept going until we walked into a large room with paintings covering the walls. Liesl and Willy Wilson and some other kids were sitting at a large table. So were two teachers, and I realized I'd seen them both before in the park. The man was the guy who'd been walking the chocolate lab who'd rubbed noses with Black Jack, and the woman was the one who'd been feeding the pigeons.

"Hey!" said Liesl, her face brightening when she saw us.

The other kids and the teachers looked at us curiously.

"Sorry for interrupting," said Adam, tugging at his hair.

"Just finishing," said Liesl.

"Are those all the kids that go here?" I asked as we were running a moment later back down the marble stairs with Liesl.

"I guess that was everyone," she said. "Willy, Robby, Zack, Kizzi, Gabriela—" She was counting on her fingers. "No, Frankie wasn't here today. Oh yeah! Frankie was at *your* school. Marisa was sick, and every time Marisa's sick Frankie goes in for her. It's an arrangement they have because Marisa wants a perfect attendance record."

Both Adam and I stopped dead in our tracks. "That was *Frankie* who was at school all day today?" I burst out laughing. "I should have guessed. It was like an alien had taken over Marisa's body."

"In a *good* way," Adam added.

"So what's going on?" asked Liesl as we stood in front of her school.

"We think the Falcons are hidden in a clock," I said, and then we told her why we thought so.

"Zowie," she said, looking at us with wide eyes.

"So we think we should start by looking in the clock in Ernie's old elevator."

Liesl nodded. "Okay, so what are we waiting for?"

By the time we got to the Ingle Building, there were a ton of people coming and going. "Rush hour," said Adam, as we stood in the crowded hallway waiting for number 10. And then as number 10 went *bing* and the doors began to open, I had the shock of my life. There was Tony, in the cranberry Ingle Building uniform.

A woman in sunglasses and a red-and-blue silk scarf tied in a knot under her chin stepped forward. "Where—where is the fellow who usually operates this elevator?" she asked.

Tony looked nervous. "He was moved into a different elevator—" he started to say.

The woman interrupted him, "He has *what*?" She plucked at the collar of the long navy blue coat she was wearing.

"I'm—I'm sorry to say there's been an accident," said Tony. "The old man—Ernie—had a bad fall last night, and he's in the hospital."

The woman swayed slightly, and Tony rushed to help her. "I'm so sorry," he said. "Is he a friend of yours?"

"This is—oh, this is terrible!" She pushed her way through the crowd and disappeared. Just at that moment, Tony spotted me. "Aiden!" he cried.

"Tony!" I said. "What are you doing here?"

"Shame about Ernie," a woman said who was holding a very small dog.

"This elevator going anywhere or what?" a man looking at his watch asked.

To make things worse, Grip appeared, striding around the corner. Adam, Liesl, and I shrank back, hoping he wouldn't notice us, and in fact he seemed too focused on Tony to notice anything else. "Let's get this car moving," he said curtly.

All the people piled into the elevator, looking slightly sheepish as if Grip had been scolding them. We piled in with them. Tony looked so funny in the uniform with gold braids on the shoulders, the Ingle Building cap perched on his thick curls, and white gloves on his hands. Finally, the last person got off, and we were the only ones left.

"And now," said Tony, "introduce me to your friends, Aiden, and tell me what brings you to the Ingle Building this afternoon."

"This is Liesl—"

"Of course, cousin Liesl, we've met!" said Tony warmly.

"And this is Adam, a friend from school."

"And we're, um, sightseeing," I said. It was way too daunting to explain the whole Gold Falcon thing to him. "Getting to know the city."

"Ha," said Tony. "Wonderful. And I suppose you're wondering what I'm doing," he said.

"Yeah," I said.

"I've been trying to figure out what to do about my voice." said Tony, "and I got to thinking about all the times I warmed up before a show in Rosie's elevator." He took off the cap and cradled it in his hands. "So I thought, what could be better than going up and down and singing all day—when no one's in here, of course, although it might be fun if they were— talk about a captive audience! So I called and got the job. I'm going to be an elevator opera-ator! Get it, OPERA-ator? It turns out they are desperate for operators because they just fired some young girl who was in here." Adam and Liesl and I looked at each other and grinned. "And all the operators are taking time off to go see Ernie in the hospital—"

"Ernie's in the *hospital*?"

Tony lowered himself onto the elevator operator's stool, his long legs sticking out in front of him. "Poor Ernie. They tell me that at about eleven last night, the night watchman thought he heard a commotion up on the terrace of the rooftop café over there on the west wing. When he went to check it out, he found Ernie on the terrace, stretched out unconscious. They rushed him off to the hospital, and Rosie went with him of course."

"That's terrible," I said.

"And what's wrong with the clock?" asked Adam.

"Well, the clock—" Tony sat up a bit.

We all stared at the clock. Where would the Gold Falcons be? At the very bottom? Behind the face? In a secret compartment somewhere in the back? I wanted to start looking.

"When I brought old Mrs. Ingle down from the Eyrie this morning, she noticed that it wasn't working," said Tony. "What's strange is that it looks as if it stopped at eleven o'clock, the same time Ernie was injured." A little shiver went through me as I stared at the face of the clock. "Mrs. Ingle was very upset about both the clock and Ernie."

The elevator had reached the lobby by now. Grip was the first person we saw when the doors opened. "You kids are here again?" His face turned red. "I told you kids—"

"They're visiting me," said Tony firmly. "I'm an uncle."

"No visiting while you're on duty," said Grip curtly, "and besides which they stole a mouse. Felix Brown never got it back."

"We didn't steal your mouse," said Liesl, standing with her hands on her hips glaring at him.

I stuck my hand in my pocket just to be sure Charles didn't choose this moment to poke his nose out, but my heart sank as I realized Charles wasn't there.

"Tony Balboni!" A man with a head of curly black hair and big black beard appeared in the hallway, carrying a large box of tools. I stared at him. His voice sounded familiar but the rest of him didn't look like anyone I'd ever seen before. Tony didn't seem to know him, either.

"I'm sorry," said Tony. "Do I know you?"

"I'm a fan," said the man. "And surprised to see you here."

The more I looked at the man, the more he looked like someone who was wearing a not very good disguise. Suddenly, I realized it was *Leo*.

"Filling in here for a while," said Tony. "Someone was needed to bring Mrs. Ingle up and down, and—"

As if saying her name made her appear, Mrs. Ingle came tapping down the hall with her cane. Ana was walking by her side. Mrs. Ingle was all dressed up in a gray suit today, her hair tightly curled. Grip darted to her side.

"How are you today, ma'am?" he asked.

"Reasonably well, Grim, for an old woman who's lost everything in life that has meaning," said Mrs. Ingle. "And speaking of being lost, have you found those Gold Falcons yet, Grim?"

"It's, er, Grip, ma'am, not Grim, and, I'm, er, working on finding the Falcons."

Her hooded eyes snapped angrily. "I can't imagine what's so difficult—"

She stopped suddenly, noticing me. "Well, Patsy! You're back! I tell you what! You come and have tea with me this afternoon."

Grip made an odd sound in his throat and Leo's jaw dropped so far I thought his fake beard was going to fall off. I made a face at Ana, as if to say help.

"Mrs. Een-go-lee," she said gently. "She's not—"

"You can bring Patsy right up to the Eyrie at five o'clock," Mrs. Ingle said to Tony. "I'll be expecting you," she added, turning back to me, "and no excuses. I'm an old woman, you can humor me." She cleared her throat and turned to Grip. "Have we been able to get hold of the clock expert, Grim?"

"Yes, of course, ma'am, and it's Gr—"

"I'm here for the clock," said Leo quietly.

Mrs. Ingle looked him up and down. "So you're the one who has looked after the clock all these years," she said. "Have we met before?"

"Yes ma'am," Leo growled.

"Well, I expect you to get to the bottom of what's wrong with it. As perhaps you know, it belonged to the very first Ingle. My husband, Edward, insisted on putting it in this elevator so we could enjoy it on the rides up and down."

"Yes ma'am," said Leo. His expression was flat and didn't show a thing.

"Now then," Mrs. Ingle said to Ana, "I want to go and check up on the kitchen staff. I'm having an important meeting with an architect tomorrow, and I want to be sure we're serving something decent for lunch. I'll see *you* at five o'clock," she said, turning and pointing the cane at me. The thousands of wrinkles in her face curved up in an odd sort of smile. She started off, her cane making a *pock, pock* sound as she moved down the hall.

Ana hung back for a second. "Don't worry," she said quickly, pressing my arm. "I'll be there."

"I don't know why she calls me Patsy," I said to Leo. He was standing there, staring at me so long and hard he was making me uncomfortable. "I heard about what happened with you and Patsy," I added. "I'm sorry."

Leo sighed deeply. "Not as sorry as I am. I should never have let her get away."

"*Who* does she think you are?" Tony asked.

"Her daughter, forty-five years ago," said Leo. He was still staring and finally he said, "You know, I *do* see it! I really do! You're tall as she was, of course, but it's your forehead and the tilt of your nose." He slapped a hand against his head and said, "Oh my word, of course!"

"What is it?" I asked.

"It's—I've just connected some dots, is all," he said. He was grinning. "And if I'm right, I'm—I'm well—this is extraordinary!" He looked around at all of us. "To be announced," he said. Glancing at Grip he added, "There's a time for everything."

Grip exclaimed, "Huh! I don't care *who* she thinks you are. Any more complaints from the clientele about stolen mouses or kids getting in the way, out you go."

I groaned inwardly. Where *had* Charles gotten to? I put a hand on Leo's arm. I wanted to know why he was in that getup. "Why," I started to ask, but he turned and put a warning finger to his lips, glancing at Grip again.

"Now, let's see what's wrong with this old geezer," he said, moving toward the clock. As he opened the glass door of the grandfather clock, Adam, Liesl, and I crowded around, watching closely, looking to see if there was a little door on the side.

"Maybe it's not working because something is getting in the way of the works." Adam suggested.

There *was* a little door, I was sure of it. I pulled Adam by the arm and pointed. He stepped in closer.

"Um, I could use a bit of room," said Leo.

"Sorry," we said, stepping back.

He fiddled with this and that. "At first glance, I don't see anything wrong with it." He turned to Grip. "Can you get some men to wrap it up and transport it to the shop?"

As soon as Grip left, I said, "Leo! What are you doing?"

Tony looked startled. "Leo? Leo Schwartz?"

"The very same," said Leo, pulling the beard away from his face for a moment. "I never come here as myself," he said. "In case I run into Mrs. Ingle. She can't abide me—and, well, it's mutual."

He reached over and patted the side of the clock. "You'd almost think this old thing stopped out of sympathy for Pa." He sighed and, kneeling, pulled a wrench from his toolbox. "I'm going to need some help getting the clock off the wall. If you all would hold it while I loosen some bolts here."

Tony, Adam, Liesl, and I stepped up to hold the clock while Leo knelt down with the wrench.

After a moment he looked up in amazement. "Look at

this!" he exclaimed. "I thought the bolts would be hard to undo, but they come off easy as pie!" Then he gave a startled yell, springing to one side and dropping the wrench. "Good grief, it's a big, fat mouse!"

"Charles!" we all shouted at the same time as nose and whiskers poked out from the bottom of the clock.

"So that's where you've been," I said. "Charles, you come here right now." Charles ran over to Tony's shoe and then up his uniformed pant leg, up his jacket, and sat on the gold braid on his shoulder, looking completely pleased with himself.

"Charles just loves you, Tony," I said.

"My biggest fan," said Tony, rubbing a hand across his face. "And maybe my *only* fan if things don't improve soon."

"Okay," said Leo, "let's pull gently now." As the clock came off the wall, Leo was on his hands and knees, his face near the bottom of the clock. "Huh!" he exclaimed. "There is a piece of paper jammed into the board at the bottom. It looks like a note of some kind."

Adam, Liesl, and I jumped as if we'd been zapped with a bolt of lightning. Sitting up, Leo held the piece of paper in one hand. It had been folded a bunch of times. He unfolded it now. It was all I could do not to grab it out of his hands. "TIME IS IN MY POCKET," he read. He raised his eyebrows at me. "A clue?" he asked, lowering his voice.

I knelt down beside him. "Does it seem familiar, Leo?"

He nodded. "Yes, I think it does." He handed it to me. TIME IS IN MY POCKET.

I pulled out my pocket watch. The words engraved on the watch seemed to jump out at me. THE BIRD OF TIME FLIES NEAR. "Oh my gosh, Leo," I said, trying not to raise my voice. Tony was looking at us oddly, and Liesl and Adam were bending over us, trying to listen. "The *watch* is part of the treasure hunt, and to think I've been carrying it around all this time! And it's what I told you, Leo, every single clue is about time or a bird."

"Yes," said Leo thoughtfully, "you are so right. Well, chew on that one for a while, Aiden. And maybe the watch has some other significance?" He turned back to the clock with a frown, pointing to the base. "Chips of wood off here. And there are a lot of scratches. Seems as if this old beauty has been moved around more than she ought to have been. I wonder what Pa's been up to."

Grip was back with several men. They wrestled the clock out of the elevator and wrapped it in padded cloths and hefted it onto a wheeled cart. As Leo started off down the hallway with it, he said, "Keep thinking, Aiden."

Adam pulled me aside. "I bet 'it' is in the clock," he whispered. "I mean the you-know-what."

Startled, I suddenly remembered Rosie's message to Ernie. Collect "it" she had said. Was "it" the collection of Gold Falcons? I thought of the way Leo had stood there just now, slapping his hand to his forehead and saying he had just connected the dots. Had he figured out the gold was in the clock and was he taking the clock away so he could collect "it" for Rosie and Ernie? Or did he want it to give to Mrs. Ingle so she would build a castle for Patsy and bring her home?

"Going up?" a man asked Tony.

"Going up," said Tony. Several people filed into the elevator, but just as the doors were closing, Grip, who was still standing in the hallway, suddenly yelled. "Hey! That mouse on your shoulder! *Where'd you get that mouse?*"

Adam, Liesl, and I managed to squeeze into the elevator just as the doors shut and Tony was already pressing buttons. The passengers in the elevator backed away from him, looking uneasily at Charles. Tony took off his hat and plopped Charles inside it. "You're a big troublemaker, Charles, you know that?" To the passengers, he said, "Not to worry, ladies and gentlemen. This is a special mouse. Likes opera and everything. Belongs to a very brilliant man, Felix Brown. You may have heard of him." He set the hat with Charles in it on his stool.

Somebody said, "Oh yes, Felix Brown and his mouse, of course," and everyone started smiling at Charles.

As the last person got out of the elevator, Adam said, "Hey, come and look at this! I was standing back here and my foot kicked against the wall and something moved." He knelt down. "There's a door here in the back wall behind where the clock was. It's like a hatch or something; it swings both ways." He held the door up with one hand and reached his arm through the opening. "But there's a solid wall behind it. What's the point of it if it doesn't go anywhere?"

Liesl went to the back of the elevator and crouched down. "The opening is big enough for a person to go through," she said. "It could lead to another secret passage."

Adam and I looked at each other. Maybe the Gold Falcons *weren't* in the clock. Maybe after all, they were hidden here behind the elevator wall.

"Stop at each floor and see if it matches up with an opening on another floor," said Adam.

"Why not?" said Tony cheerfully. "Until someone calls for me."

Adam stood at the back. Each time we reached a new floor, he kicked the little swinging door with the heel of his shoe. Just as we reached the 86th floor, Adam cried out, "Bingo!" He knelt and stuck his arm into the opening. "There's definitely an open space back here, and I can feel a floor."

Charles popped out of Tony's hat, leaped down to the floor, and scampered across to Adam. He raised himself up on his hind legs, his ears and nose twitching a mile a minute. "Better grab him, Adam!" Tony said, but it was too late. In a flash, Charles disappeared into the black hole.

"Maybe he hasn't gone very far," Liesl said, kneeling next to Adam.

"I think we should find out what's in there," I said. We were up high now, closer to the falcon on top of the building. Maybe the important word in THE BIRD OF TIME FLIES NEAR was bird. "Charles has never led us wrong in the past."

25

"Hang on," said Tony. "You're not going in there alone and certainly not without a light." He stood up and, reaching into a box marked EMERGENCY, brought out a flashlight. "And I better turn off this elevator. I would not like it going anywhere while we're in that secret whatever it is. I do not want to be stranded somewhere inside the walls of the Ingle Building." He flicked a switch and then he said, "All right, go on, who's first? I'll try to follow with the light."

As Adam plunged through the swinging door, I thought about how only a few days ago he had been scared to go through the under-the-park tunnel; now he was the one who had found this opening, and he was going in first.

In a moment we heard him say, "There's a lot of room back here."

Liesl plunged in next, and I followed her. From the sounds of grunting and groaning behind me and the way the beam of the flashlight kept bouncing around, Tony didn't seem to be having too easy a time.

"I don't think this secret passage was built for opera singers," he said as he finally made it through. He swung the flashlight around. "I'd say we were in some kind of well between floors, and Mrs. Ingle's Eyrie must be above us."

"There's a ladder," said Adam.

The beam of the flashlight rested on a ladder built into the wall. It appeared to go up and up and up. Charles was sitting on one of the rungs. His eyes shone like two lamps. He squeaked and then scampered up the ladder.

"Oh Charles," I said with a sigh, "will you please just come back?"

"That ladder must lead somewhere," Liesl said.

"I was afraid you might think something like that," said Tony.

"I'll go up first with the flashlight, and then I'll hold it for you while you guys come up," said Adam.

He took the flashlight from Tony and started up.

"I'm at the top!" Several minutes later, Adam's voice floated down from way above us. The flashlight beam spread itself feebly down the length of the ladder, not even reaching the bottom rungs.

"I'll be right behind you," said Tony, as if he could sense my nervousness. "That way if you fall, I'll fall, too, and you'll have something soft to land on. And then you can tell me why we're doing this."

"We're looking for Things," said Liesl. She was on her way up the ladder. Probably not a good time to tell her to keep her mouth shut.

"Not gold Things by any chance?" Tony asked.

"Too hard to explain right now," I said. I put my foot on the first rung and, reaching up, began to haul myself up.

The beam from the flashlight Adam was holding grew stronger and now, looking up, I could see Liesl disappearing through an opening in a platform made of long boards that stretched across the open space.

"You're almost there, Liesl," said Adam. He was lying, belly down, on the boards. His arm was hanging down over the edge as he held the flashlight. "Just scramble over here now, but watch your head. There's a big plywood box or something like that above us."

I heard Liesl scrambling. "Made it," she said.

Breathing hard and sweating like crazy, I managed to pull myself up through the opening.

"Okay, pull yourself over here." As I scrambled off the ladder and onto the boards, I could see the box Adam had been talking about. There was hardly any room between us and the bottom of it. I lay on my back next to Liesl, gasping in the hot, stuffy air.

"I bet the go—I mean, the Things, are up here somewhere," said Liesl.

Tony's hands appeared on the rung above the opening in the platform; I started to move over to make room for him, a little worried about how this was going to work. But as Tony's head popped up and he rested his arms on the platform, he said, "That's okay, stay where you are, Aiden. There's no way I'm leaving this ladder. Phew! That was a workout. So, now what?"

Adam swung the flashlight around. "See those electric cables over there? I bet the box is an industrial elevator that goes up inside the mountain so they can change the spotlights that shine on the falcon and stuff like that."

"Shine the light up again," I said. "I thought I saw a metal ring on it." Adam swung the beam up. "We have a ring like that on our door that opens up into the hayloft of the barn," I said. "You pull down on it and the door opens and these little stairs swing down."

I actually managed to do a half sit-up and grabbed the ring and then let the top half of my body relax, hoping my weight would release the door, but nothing happened. "It's stuck or locked or something. Oh—I see a lock now. Too bad."

"We could try forcing it," said Adam. "If all three of us pull on it—"

Just as I began reaching for the ring again, there was a loud whirring from below us, and the entire platform began to vibrate.

Adam pointed the beam down, and it caught the top of the elevator. Then we watched it going down . . . and down . . . and down . . . until we couldn't see it anymore. For several moments, the whirring and the vibrating continued, but it grew fainter and fainter. And then everything was dead quiet and still.

Tony groaned. "How is that possible? I turned off the power. You saw me do it."

"Someone must have gotten in at the 86th floor," said Adam.

"But the elevator shouldn't open from the outside with the power off. Grip managed to tell me that much in my five-minute training session this morning."

"This is not good," said Adam.

"Holy mackerel!" Tony suddenly yelled at the top of his lungs, and his yelling made me yell, and my yell made Liesl yell, and there was a whizzing sound of something falling rapidly through the air, ending with a terrible shatter. And then it was very dark.

"I dropped the flashlight," Adam said in a small voice.

"Yes," said Tony.

"When you yelled like that," said Adam, "it startled me."

"Well, Charles startled me," said Tony. "He ran across my hand—at least I think it was Charles. It could have been—"

"Don't *say* it, Tony." I shuddered.

"Come on," he said. "We've reached a dead end here. That elevator is going to have to come back up eventually, and we better be in the right spot when it does. Let's climb down and get on some firm ground. Come on, kids, I'll help you get off the platform."

I felt the dark press against me, and the palms of my hands were sweaty. And then suddenly there was the tiniest bit of light. Tony was holding open his cell phone. I reached out and felt Tony's big hands grab on to me.

"You slide past me and go on down," he said, "and I'll wait here for Liesl and Adam."

Down I went, rung by rung. Once all four of us were down, we held open our cell phones, and we were able to get a sense of where the edge of the elevator shaft was. "Careful of broken glass," said Tony.

We sat on the floor, pressed together. Tony was next to me, and I was glad to feel his big, reassuring presence. I closed my cell phone, wanting to save the batteries.

"The elevator is bound to come back up," he said again. "And when it does, we'll dive for the door."

I wondered if anyone would hear us calling for help in here. If they didn't, we'd start to get hungry and then hungrier, and then thirsty and then thirstier, and the *rats* . . . the *rats* . . .

Suddenly, Tony started singing. He sang one single note carried on a huge breath, and it broke into my panic. And then he started to sing a song in Italian; the words were full of warm vowels, like glowing little embers. When that song ended, Tony started in on another, a funny one this time, with peppery short notes and lots of ha ha ha's that made me laugh.

And then I felt something at my fingertips, something small and metal. I opened my cell phone. In the light I saw it was a key. I turned it around and around in my hand.

"Tony!" I shook his arm.

Tony stopped singing. "Had enough, have you?"

"No, no, it's not that. I love your singing, Tony. It—it makes everything seem like it's going to be okay. And you didn't croak once."

"That's true," said Tony, sounding pleased. "I didn't even *think* about croaking, to be honest."

"I never thought I would like opera," said Adam, "but I liked that. Why'd you stop him, Aiden?"

"I found a key," I said.

"A key? Where?"

"Right here, on the floor.," I said. "It might belong to the door in the floor of that box or industrial elevator or whatever it is, and if it is we can get out of here."

26

"I'm out of here," said Adam, leaping up.

"Whoa—steady there, cowboy," said Tony. "We don't want you lurching over the edge."

I could hear the swish of Adam's khakis as he headed for the ladder. I scrambled to my feet slowly. I was only too aware of that empty blackness just a few feet away from us. It made my legs wobble just thinking about it. I found Liesl's arm and grabbed onto it. Just as Tony stood up, Adam yelled, and there was a sickening sound of a body bumping down the ladder.

"Oh brother," said Liesl.

"Ow, ow, ow!" Adam was moaning. We made our way over to him. Tony was crouched beside him, holding his cell phone open over him. Adam's face was crumpled in pain, and he was clutching his ankle.

"My hands slipped, and my ankle—"

"Can you put any weight on it?" Tony asked. He tried hauling Adam up, but Adam started moaning again.

I wanted to kick Adam for not being more careful. "Good move," said Liesl, saying out loud what I was thinking.

Then Tony said, "I guess we go back to waiting."

"You guys should go," said Adam in a small voice.

"We can't leave you here by yourself," said Tony.

I jammed the key into my pocket and took a breath. "I'll go up there," I said.

"I'll come with you," said Liesl.

No one said anything for a moment. And then Tony said, "All right. I'll stay here with Adam. Come on, Adam, try to get comfortable. Lean your back against the wall and try to think pleasant thoughts." He stood up for a moment between Liesl and me and circled a big arm around each of us. "And you, girls, climb slowly and carefully and don't take unnecessary risks."

"Sing again," I said. "It'll make us brave."

Liesl went ahead of me. I waited for her to get a few rungs above me and, as I began to climb, I heard Tony settle himself on the floor. He began to sing again, and this time it was as if his big voice was pushing me up the ladder.

But then from far below, the whirring, grinding sound came back; I could feel the ladder begin to vibrate as I held onto it.

"It's coming back!" Tony shouted. "The elevator's coming back!"

Liesl and I hadn't gotten very far. In just a few seconds we were back standing beside Tony. He was on his feet now, his cell phone open. "Crawl over to the edge," he ordered. "Be ready to dive through the opening. Go on, Adam, you go first."

The noise grew closer and closer, and the ground we were standing on began to shake. It was if a monster was approaching.

"Go on, Adam, go!" Tony yelled. He practically picked up Adam, swinging him through the door. I went next, knocking my elbows painfully on the floor as I landed on the other side. Half a minute later, Liesl came rolling in, and then, finally, Tony flopped through like a big fish.

The light was almost blinding, and as I sat up, blinking, and nursing my elbows, it took me a minute to take in the faces of the two people who were staring down at us. Gradually, I realized I was looking at the big, red, beefy face of Grip above his cranberry-colored uniform and the rumpled face of Felix Brown.

"I told you they were up here," said Grip. "What were you doing in there?"

"You mean to say you brought the elevator down, knowing full well we were trapped in there?" Tony was furious, waving his big arms and shouting. "You purposely endangered our lives. We could have fallen down that shaft!" He was on his feet, headed for the control panel.

"Whaddya think you're doing?" Grip snarled and put out a hand to stop Tony.

"What do you think *you're* doing?" Tony still was shouting. "We have an injured kid here."

I looked at Adam, still on the floor next to me, cradling his ankle in his hands. He was a mess. There were cobwebs all over him. I looked down at myself. I didn't look much better.

"I asked you a question," said Grip. "What were you doing in there behind the elevator? You're supposed to be operating this elevator, not playing hide-and-seek."

"We went after the mouse," said Tony.

"They *were* after the mouse!" said Felix with enormous relief. "I told you!"

"Huh!" said Grip. "Then where is it? We're not going nowhere till we see that mouse."

"Oh my gosh," said Adam, disgusted. "All this for a mouse?"

And that's when I saw a familiar shape poking out of Grip's pocket. My *hat*. What was Grip doing with my hat? And then I got it. While looking for Charles the other day up in that café, Grip had been called in, and he'd found my hat and then he'd found the clue.

They're not looking for a mouse, I thought; they're looking for the *gold*, and they think we have it. The mouse is just an excuse.

"All right, so cough up the mouse."

"The mouse has a mind of his own," said Tony. "I don't know where he is right now. Last we knew, he was in there." He pointed toward the back of the elevator.

"Yeah—so you can go back in there, then, and start looking," Grip said grimly.

"We are not going back in there," said Tony, "and you can't make us."

"Yeah? Then we can just stay here, can't we? And as for you, little lady—" Grip turned toward me. "I believe you got some information—"

"I don't know what you're talking about." My heart had started pumping madly. I had formed an idea.

"Don't you, now?"

I made sure the key was still in my pocket and then inched my way back toward the swinging door.

Grip pulled the hat out of his pocket and shook it. "You know something about the writing in this?"

I dropped to the floor and made the plunge. On the way through, something furry brushed against my face.

"HEY!" I heard Grip shouting as I frantically pulled myself forward, banging up my elbows again. I kicked with my feet as if I were swimming. As soon as I could, I jumped up and threw myself at the place I was pretty sure by now held the ladder. My legs were shaking and my hands were sweaty as I started to climb, sure that Grip would be coming after me. I didn't want to fall the way Adam had, so I gripped each rung so hard my fingers hurt.

I had the sensation that I was underwater like that time when I was about four, before I could swim, when I'd fallen off the dock and into the pond and everything had gone black and I thought I'd never see the light again. Pops had reached down and pulled me up by the straps of my overalls.

He couldn't rescue me now. I had to get to the top by myself.

Climbing, one rung after another, and coming up through the platform at last, I hauled myself onto it and flipped over so I was lying on my back. The wooden boards jounced under the weight of my body. I had to curl slightly to get the key out of my pocket, and then I did a sit-up, like before, hanging on with one hand to the metal ring. I reached up with my other hand and tried to fit the key in the lock. It didn't seem to want to go in.

I thought I heard a noise below me. Maybe Grip was halfway up the ladder by now.

Concentrating on keeping my hand steady, the bit of metal finally slipped into the slot. "Please work," I prayed. The key turned with a little click. I grabbed the ring and pulled, and a step swung down. I hauled myself up and through the opening and then I sat up on the floor. Pulling up my legs so they were out of the way, I found a cord and tugged. The step retracted, and the door shut with a snap. My hand was shaking so hard I could barely hold onto the key, but I managed to stick it in the slot of the lock and turn it and lock it again.

Then I lay flat on my back and shut my eyes and just breathed, waiting for the trembling to stop. Just as I was beginning to calm down, a loud noise almost had me jumping out of my skin. I sat up. It was the elevator, whirring and grinding, thunderously at first and then more and more faintly until it stopped altogether.

So—they were going down in the elevator.

I peeled the key off the palm of my hand where it had been pressing into it and put it in my pocket. For the first time, it occurred to me that maybe this was the key Rosie had given me to give to Ernie. I sat up, startled. In the story, the girl was climbing the mountain looking for gold. And here I was, practically on top of the mountain. THE BIRD OF TIME FLIES NEAR. Was this where the Gold Falcons were?

The elevator was a box that had a floor, four walls, and no ceiling; it was resting inside the bottom of the mountain. Sheets of pink granite supported by huge beams rose up around me on four sides, like a pyramid, not quite coming to a point.

The whole thing, elevator and mountain, swayed slightly, and I thought about how high up I was. Something like eighty-eight stories high. I didn't know how many feet that was, but it was a lot.

I wiped my sweaty palms on my skirt. Gold Falcons could very well be up here, but I had no idea where to look and no energy left. I just wanted to get out of there. I got up and opened the door, and then I was outside the elevator in a dark and dingy hallway. I had to grope my way down to the end of it to find another door. To my relief, it opened and led to a set of stairs. As I started going down, someone was coming up. Slowly and carefully, one cautious step at a time. Mrs. Ingle was looking up at me.

"Oh Patsy," she gasped, "I thought I heard a noise up here, and it turns out to be you, so it must be time for tea.

I commend you for finding your way up here. My elevator doesn't seem to be working."

I had completely forgotten about Mrs. Ingle and her invitation to tea. I was grateful, now, because it was the best reason for being where she had found me.

She reached up and grasped my arm. "Yes, well, it's dandy to see you and don't tell on me. I was just sneaking up to take a look at my poor, lonely birdy. He's lost his mate, you know. But you're here now, so do let's go down for tea."

She turned around on the stairs and, gripping the railing, began to make her way back down the few stairs she'd come up. While her back was turned, I opened my cell phone. Five missed messages from Adam. Three from Mom. I tried calling. No signal.

We came to a landing. Mrs. Ingle pulled open a door, and we stepped into a hallway with a honey-colored carpet and wallpaper with gold flecks in it. We went through another door into a huge room filled with dazzling light. Two corners of the enormous room were made up of giant windows. I felt a little dizzy standing there, looking out on the world spread out far below us.

Two flowery couches faced the windows and at the other end of the room was a dining table, the top polished and gleaming, reflecting the chandelier that hung above it. The wooden chairs reminded me of something out of the Middle Ages. Falcons were carved into the backs, and there were cranberry-red cushions on them with gold tassels hanging down at the corners.

Spread out on top of the table were a couple of large sheets of white paper covered with black-and-white drawings of a large building with turrets and towers poking up through funny-looking trees. At the bottom in big, block letters was written DESIGN FOR PATSY'S CASTLE. My stomach knotted. And then, practically taking up one whole wall, was the largest portrait I'd ever seen in my life. It was of a lady in a pink gown, all satin and silk, only it wasn't just pink, it was cream and rose; she had diamonds around her long, creamy neck, and long, white gloves on her arms, and she was carrying deep red roses. Her skin and her cheeks were all pink and rose and cream, too, but her lips were a rich red and she had dark hair that shone and blue eyes that seemed to sparkle like the diamonds.

I didn't know what to say. I was stunned.

"You'll never guess, my dear, who that might be," said Mrs. Ingle.

I turned to look at her. The eyes were the giveaway. "It's you," I said.

"Commissioned by my husband." Her voice caught, and she seemed unable to say another word.

I put my hand on her arm and, before I could even think about what I was saying, I said, "I know how it feels, Mrs. Ingle. My father died, too. It's like—it's like all of a sudden you fall off the dock and you think you're going to drown."

She grasped my hand with one of her hands. It felt very cold. "Falling off the dock," she said. "Yes, but—" She seemed to focus on me for the first time. "How old are you, my dear? You're awfully young to have lost your father."

"Like your kids were," I said.

"My kids." She looked confused for a moment.

"I'm not really Patsy, you know."

Mrs. Ingle took her hand off mine and held it against her face for a moment, covering her eyes. Then she walked over to a little desk in one corner of the room where there was an old-fashioned black telephone. She picked up the receiver and spoke into it. "We're ready for tea now, Ana," she said crisply. "Yes, that's right, she's here." She put down the receiver. "Let's go sit down, shall we?"

I took one look at the flowered couch Mrs. Ingle was headed for and then looked down at myself. I was filthy. "Mrs. Ingle," I said, "I need to wash up first."

"Certainly, my dear," she said. "Just go through that door and down that hallway. There's a washroom at the end on the right."

It was a relief to use the bathroom and wash my face and hands in the sink, but I felt bad using the little white towels with flowers embroidered on them. As I headed back out, I noticed bedrooms along the hallway. Poking my head into one of them, I saw a dresser with a lacy doily on it, little china figures of cats and dogs all over it. This must have been Patsy's room. I couldn't help going in. There were paintings of birds on the walls. Patsy had liked animals, just like I did.

On the dresser beside the china figures there were some photographs in small frames. I went over to take a look. There was one of a man and a woman—he was nice-looking with a mustache, looking very serious compared to the woman who was wrapped in a fur coat, her face bright with a dazzling smile. Edward and Felicity, I guessed. And then there was another set of photographs in a pair of frames that were hinged together. A boy and a girl.

I stared at the girl. Patsy? And *did* I look like her? It was an old black-and-white photograph and a little blurry. There was a mirror on the dresser. I glanced at myself in it and then looked at the photograph again. We did both have these high foreheads and maybe our noses were sort of the same. Our hair was different, though, that's for sure. Hers was in long braids.

Then I studied the boy. I supposed this must be Bertie and, honestly, with my short hair I looked more like him than the girl. He was really cute. He had a mischievous smile with a dimple on his chin—but then I realized I'd seen this boy before. Many times. There was a portrait of him hanging on the wall next to the grandfather clock in the living room of the farmhouse. It was almost the same likeness as this photograph—in fact, the painting could have been made from this photograph. But the painting at home was of my grandpa Farmer.

I stared and stared at the boy. There wasn't that much light in the room, and people in photographs from the old days could all look alike. Maybe I was mistaken. Or maybe I had always been mistaken in thinking the painting was of Grandpa Farmer. Maybe he actually was someone in the Balboni family.

My brain felt cobwebby. I put the frame down and went back to Mrs. Ingle's living room.

28

"There you are," said Mrs. Ingle. She led me over to one of the flowered couches that had a shiny brass coffee table in front of it. I sat down on the poofy cushions and then she sat down two poofy cushions over from me.

"Now then," she said, "I know, of course, that you are not really Patsy. I'm old, my dear, but not entirely gaga. It is just that you look enough like Patsy to bring me some comfort. But, now, my dear, what really is your name?"

"Aiden," I said. "Aiden Farmer."

"Aiden," she repeated. "Your first name conjures up warriors from another time. *Are* you a warrior, my dear?"

"My dad used to say I was a scrappy little kid," I said.

Mrs. Ingle laughed, a sort of tinkling laugh, like the sound an icicle makes if you knock it to the ground. "And your last name . . . is . . . Farmer?"

"Yup, and the funny thing is, on my father's side of the family, they always were farmers."

"Yes, indeed, and they must have been so a long way back to have a name like that. And are you a farmer, too?"

"I wish," I said.

Mrs. Ingle didn't say anything for a moment. She turned

the rings on her old fingers around and around. "And what," she finally said, "is so compelling about the farming life?"

"It . . . just . . . it makes *sense*." So many thoughts and images welled up, I didn't know where to begin. "You're a part of things. The seasons. They matter. The weather. It matters. If it rains or doesn't rain, it makes a difference. You always know where your food is coming from." I punched the poofy pillow, struggling to find the right words. "And on a farm, everything smells good—the cows and the hay and the silage."

Mrs. Ingle wrinkled her nose. "Surely *silage* doesn't smell good."

I blurted out, "You should know, your son was a farmer."

Mrs. Ingle's sharp blue eyes clouded for a moment. I thought she might have asked me how I knew about Bertie, but she only said, "Yes, and I could never understand why. It was a great sorrow to me, his going off like that . . ."

Ana came in carrying a big silver tray. I was so glad to see her, and she winked when she saw me. She set the tray on the table without even banging it, which I thought was pretty impressive considering it had an enormous silver tea-pot on it, two cups and saucers, two spoons, a little silver pitcher of milk, a silver bowl of sugar cubes, a small dish with slices of lemon, a large plate heaped with cookies and little cakes, and cloth napkins in silver napkin rings. Phew.

"I'll have you pour out for us, Ana." Ana gave me a nice, big smile and then hefted up the teapot and started pouring tea into the cups.

Mrs. Ingle picked up a napkin ring and pulled out the napkin and put it in her lap. I got the hint and did the same thing. The napkin ring was pretty, with feathery, fancy initials engraved into it—the letters *P R I*. Patsy Ingle, I thought.

"Milk or sugar, Miss?" asked Ana, winking at me again.

"She can do that for herself, Ana," said Mrs. Ingle.

"Will that be all, then, Mrs. Een-go-lee?"

"Yes, thank you, Ana."

Ana gave me another smile and left the room. I wished she could have stayed. I had a feeling nothing could go wrong as long as Ana was there. I reached over and nervously poured milk into my cup. I was afraid of being a klutz. I took a deep breath and, picking up a pair of little silver tongs for pinching up the sugar cubes, plopped four into my tea.

"When I saw your young face, Aiden," said Mrs. Ingle, putting a slice of lemon into her cup, "I was reminded of a time when things were—happy. When my Edward was still alive." I glanced sideways at her. She looked so sad, I couldn't help feeling a little sorry for her. "And after he died, things were never the same. I was so worried, you see, about keeping the business going. It wasn't all that common for a woman in those days to be in the position that I was in, and I had so much to learn. I'm afraid I neglected the children. I'm not proud of that, of course, but I'm not the monster they make me out to be."

As I listened, I poked at my sugar cubes, watching them crumble and cave in as they dissolved.

"And then . . . there were so many disappointments. My fault, of course, for not paying better attention." Her tone of voice suddenly changed. "That ridiculous business of Patsy falling in love with that unsuitable boy."

She didn't look sad anymore, and I stopped feeling sorry for her. I had my cup halfway raised to my mouth. "It was *not* ridiculous," I blurted out, waving my cup in the air, and suddenly there was hot tea dripping everywhere. "Oh my gosh!" I said, crashing down the cup and dabbing at everything with my napkin. "I'm so sorry, Mrs. Ingle."

Mrs. Ingle reached over and patted my knee. "Don't worry about a thing, my dear. Patsy always used to spill her tea, too. It was quite a joke with us."

I clenched my teeth. "It was *not* ridiculous," I said again.

"No," said Mrs. Ingle softly. "I know that now." Her voice had changed again. "I just sometimes tell myself that to make myself feel that I was in the right all those years ago. Pride, you know." She leaned toward me slightly. "You are a plainspoken young woman. Most people tiptoe around me, afraid to speak their minds. Do you know, Aiden, even though it seemed so important all those years ago, for the life of me I can't really remember anymore what all the fuss was about. More than anything else before I die, I wish I could see my daughter again and tell her that I have never regretted anything so much in my life." Her hand was trembling, and she had to put down her cup. "There. I've said it. And I have not made such a confession to a living soul in all these years. Where did you come from, Aiden Farmer, that you should have wrung such a truth from me?"

I had no idea how to answer that one. I picked up the napkin ring. Looking at the initials, I asked, "What was Patsy's middle name?"

"Rain," she said.

I couldn't help laughing. "*Rain*? That's a funny name."

"Rain was *my* name before I married. Patsy never much liked it, poor girl, because sometimes when she was being a sourpuss we would call her Rainy-Day."

"Rainy-Day!" I said, laughing again. "I sure wouldn't like being called that."

"There were many things I said and did that I am sure she didn't like," said Mrs. Ingle. She pressed her lips together and sank back into the poofy pillows. "I know that I wasn't the best mother, but someone had to keep this place going. I know that I was a spoiled, overprivileged girl, but I pulled myself together and rose to the challenge." Mrs. Ingle stopped speaking and closed her eyes. "Sometimes just thinking about everything I've accomplished makes me tired. But," and her eyes flew open again, "I'm not finished yet. I have a castle to build—yes, I have a castle to build."

Now her eyes were wet and glittery.

Ana came in at that moment. "How are we doing?" she asked, but then, stepping closer, her voice full of concern, she said, "Mrs. Een-go-lee, you are looking a little tired."

Mrs. Ingle waved a hand at Ana. "I would like to look at the family albums, Ana. Do you know where they are? I know this girl looks just like Patsy when she was this age, and I want to prove it to her."

"Perhaps another day, Mrs. Een-go-lee," said Ana, as she began to clear up the tea things.

"I can come back soon," I said. I was actually beginning to feel desperate to leave. I wanted to know what had happened to the others, and it had been a long day of scrambling up ladders.

"Perhaps I am a little tired," said Mrs. Ingle. "But you will come back, won't you? They all—they all fly away—and they don't return." Her face looked terrible, so sad I could barely look at her.

"Now, now, Mrs. Een-go-lee," said Ana in a soothing tone of voice, "my husband tells me the Bird Lady is replacing Lady Peregrine's damaged wing feathers, and she will be flying back here in no time."

"Yes, Ana, that's nice," said Mrs. Ingle.

"And Sadie is coming in for the evening," said Ana. "She will fix you a light supper and then you must get some rest. You go ahead down, Aiden, and meet Fernando, and I will join you as soon as I can."

With some effort, Mrs. Ingle pushed herself off the couch and stood up. "I shall walk you to the elevator to see if that clock has been repaired," she said.

29

Mrs. Ingle and I stood in front of the elevator doors, and I pressed the call button. For a moment I had an awful thought. What if for some reason the elevator doors opened and Grip was standing there? The thought made me weak in the knees. I was glad Mrs. Ingle was with me.

The doors opened. Tony and I both yelled when we saw each other, and he rushed out and threw his arms around me.

"Well!" said Mrs. Ingle. "You must be old friends!"

"Oh yes," said Tony, still keeping one arm circled about me. "And you will be happy to see *your* old friend, the clock, is back in its place, Mrs. Ingle."

Mrs. Ingle nodded. "I do see. And it really is working?"

"Yes, indeed. Le—" he stopped himself in time. "The clock repairman brought it back just before I came up here. It seems it started again just as mysteriously as it stopped. He couldn't find a single thing wrong with it." A crafty look passed over Tony's face, the same expression he had had when he played the part of Figaro, and he was figuring out how to fool someone. "Do you know, Mrs. Ingle, the clock repairman believes the clock stopped working because it missed Ernie?"

Mrs. Ingle looked startled.

"There have been several very well-known cases of this happening."

"If there is any chance at all that this clock has stopped out of sympathy for Ernie," said Mrs. Ingle quickly, "we must have him come back. And what do we hear about Ernie?"

Tony smiled. "Good news on that front, too, Mrs. Ingle. He came to a few hours ago, and they say he is sitting up and talking. The only things wrong with him are a broken leg and a few cracked ribs. He's a tough old bird, all right."

"Well, I'm glad to hear it," said Mrs. Ingle. "It would be hard, after all, to imagine life without him. I have felt at sixes and sevens since he's been gone and, while you are far better than that chit of a girl who was in here before you, I shall be very glad to have him back." She suddenly peered at Tony intently. "Do you know, young man, you have an uncanny resemblance to an up-and-coming opera singer I admire very much, except that he seems to suffer from a bad case of nerves. It would be a shame, I think, if he did not immediately take steps to cure those nerves."

As Tony's face turned as red as the cranberry outfit he was wearing, a call button lit up. "I have to be going, Mrs. Ingle."

"Better hop in there, Patsy," said Mrs. Ingle. "Oh dear—I mean Aiden Farmer and, Aiden Farmer, I expect you to come back and see me soon."

As soon as the doors closed, Tony sank down on the stool and took off the cap. "I was so worried about you, Aiden."

"I got that hatch unlocked, Tony, and it did go up into an elevator that goes way up inside the mountain—and then as I was coming back down the stairs, I ran into Mrs. Ingle. She was expecting me to come and have tea with her. I couldn't get out of it." I took a deep breath and leaned against a wall, suddenly feeling so beat I could hardly stand. "But I was worried about you and Liesl and Adam, too. What happened?"

"Charles happened," said Tony with a grin. "Just as you bolted out of there, Charles scampered in and ran right up my leg and sat on my shoulder as if he'd never caused a bit of trouble. Felix demanded I hand him over. When he saw I was happy to do that, he relaxed and told Grip everything was all right now. But Grip kept insisting he wasn't going to let anyone go until you were found because you know where the Gold Falcons are. *Do* you, Aiden?"

"Oh good grief. *No.*"

"He wanted to hold us as hostages until you were found, but, happily, Felix had the upper hand and told him not to be silly. Felix said you couldn't possibly know—he, himself, has been looking for them for years and has never found them." Tony took off his hat and ran his fingers through his hair. "Felix told Liesl to crawl through that blasted door again. She hollered out your name for about five minutes and went up and down the ladder but didn't see you. We figured you'd gotten away okay. So we went down to the lobby, and Felix and Charles went off—I did feel sorry for Charles as I said good-bye to him—I had a sense he was a little depressed about having to go back to Felix. His little ears sort of folded down and his whiskers got all droopy. Grip was pretty grumpy by this time, but he finally went off, muttering to himself. And then Adam suddenly got very antsy and said he had to go home and do his homework. I said we ought to take him to the emergency room, but he said he was fine and hobbled off. He seemed to be able to walk reasonably well, so I think he's okay. And Liesl was going to wait around for you, but it kept getting later and later, so she went home."

We reached the lobby, and the doors opened. The lady in the scarf and sunglasses was standing in the hallway, a bunch of bags slung over her shoulder.

"I came to find out about Ernie," she said anxiously.

"I'm happy to tell you he is much improved," said Tony. "They say he's sitting up and talking."

"Talking!" said the lady with a laugh. "Then he must be okay."

"He's a friend of yours?" Tony asked.

"He was like a father to me," she said, her voice quavering. "I don't know what I'd do if anything ever happened to him—"

"Here," said Tony, taking her arm and guiding her over to the chair in the corner of the elevator. "I don't have any customers right now. Come sit down a minute."

The woman sat for a minute, struggling to find a tissue in one of her bags. Then she said, "Can you take me down to the parking garage now?" she asked. "Level three?"

Tony nodded, pressing the button. "He's a good man, Ernie. They don't make 'em like that anymore."

"Oh *yes*," said the woman, pressing a hand to her heart, "you are *so* right!"

"Well, here we are," said Tony, opening the doors.

The woman took off her sunglasses and dabbed at her eyes with the tissue. "Oh here I am sniffling like a baby. Ernie would have teased me for sure. 'Now, now, what's to cry about, Rainy-Day?' he would have said." She put the sunglasses back on. "Thank you so much for the good news about Ernie," and she was out of the elevator before I could say a word.

30

"I have to follow her," I shouted.

"Aiden?" Tony was looking at me strangely.

"Give me five minutes," I said, darting out of the elevator. "Tell Ana I'll meet her at the cab."

Rainy-Day—Patsy—was tall and her scarf was bright. As I raced across the garage, I spotted her easily. She was walking quickly and, to my complete surprise, she stopped in front of the door marked ELECTRICAL, NO ADMITTANCE. Looking around nervously, she opened the door, hitched the bags over her shoulder, and disappeared.

I raced to the door, but a pair of security guards walked by and chose that very door to lean against while they talked. Without bothering to wait for the elevator, I raced upstairs and outside, and there was Fernando's cab. I wrenched open the backdoor and dove in.

"Aiden!" Fernando, Melo, and Ana all turned to me.

"I have to try to catch her—that woman," I said.

"Which—who? What's going on?" asked Fernando.

Before I answered him, I was on my cell phone, calling Liesl.

"Aiden Farmer!" Liesl squealed on the other end. "What happened to you?"

"I'll explain later," I said. "But right now I have to tell you something. You know that woman in the elevator we saw, the one with the scarf and sunglasses—the one who was asking for Ernie? She'll be coming out of the secret passage at your end. Go down and wait for her and call me when she comes out. And then follow her and tell me where she goes. We'll meet you over on that side." Then I said to Fernando, "Can we drive to the other side of the park, to the entrance closest to the tree house?"

Fernando pulled out into the street. "*Minha filha*, tell us now what is going on."

I swallowed hard, trying to catch my breath. "I found Mrs. Ingle's daughter, Patsy, and I have to talk to her." Ana, turning around in her seat, looked shocked. "She's coming through the park, and she should be by the tree house in about—I don't know how long it will take her—fifteen minutes? And then Liesl can trail her," I said. "Please hurry, Fernando!"

There was a lot of traffic, and the cab seemed to be moving along at a snail's pace. Then I felt a squirt of panic. Mom would be wondering where I was. I quickly called her on the cell phone.

"Aiden!" I could hear the relief in her voice.

"I'm with Fernando and Ana and Melo," I said. "I'll be home soon."

"How soon?"

"Pretty soon. I'll call you."

Then I called Liesl again. "Is she out yet?"

"No," said Liesl. "And who is this dame? Does she have the gold?"

"No, she's—"

"Hold on, wait, the door is opening—" There was a pause. We were stuck at the longest red light in the history of the world. *Come on come on,* I thought, digging my nails into the palm of my hand.

"She's out," Liesl said in a low voice. "Tall dame, right? Carrying a bunch of bags?"

"Yes," I said. The red light changed, and Fernando was moving forward again.

"I'll just trot along a little behind her, talking on my cell phone—it won't seem like I'm paying any attention to her. So *what* happened to you?"

"Liesl, I'll explain later, I really will—"

"Whoa, she walks fast! She's as tall as a giraffe or something."

"Fernando, please hurry."

"Trying, *minha filha,* I am trying! Here we go—can't park here, though. You get out, I'll keep driving around the block."

"We're at the gate," I said into the phone as I opened the door.

"We're almost there, too," said Liesl.

I slid out, slammed the door. The next second, Melo had flung himself out of the cab, too, and was standing next to me.

"Melo!" Ana called to him, halfway out the door herself.

"I want to be with Aiden!" he said, running for me.

Cars were honking. Ana pulled herself back into the cab, yelling, "We'll go around the block!"

I could see a woman walking rapidly toward us, but she wasn't the lady in the long coat and scarf. She was the lady I'd seen at the soccer game, with the long white hair and T-shirt and jeans—the one who'd told the story—

"Bird Lady!" Melo yelled, running toward her.

The woman stopped and bent down to greet him. "Hey, buddy, what are you doing here all by yourself in the park?"

"I'm with Aiden," he said.

I walked over to her. She looked startled when she saw me. "Didn't I just see you? In the elevator? Oh! Now I know why you looked familiar—you were with Melo at the soccer game."

"Can we go somewhere and talk?" I asked. "I'm Fortunato Balboni's great-granddaughter. My name is Aiden Farmer—and, well, I know who you are."

Liesl, who had been standing only a few yards away, pretending to yak into her cell phone, came bursting over to us. *"Who?* Who is she?"

"She's the Bird Lady," said Melo. "She fixes broken birds and tells stories. You can finish the story now! The one about looking for gold!"

Bird Lady, Rainy-Day, Patsy leaned down and ruffled Melo's hair. "Soon," she said, "but you are—" She looked at me curiously. "Fortunato Balboni's great-granddaughter?"

"And I'm her cousin so I'm related to him, too," said Liesl, and then to me she asked again, *"Who* is she?"

I paused a moment, staring at the woman I was supposed to look like. Well, she was a lot older and I couldn't exactly see it. Then I said, "She's Patricia Rain Ingle."

"You know," said Bird Lady, Rainy-Day, Patsy, her eyes very wide, "I think it would be a *very* good idea to find some place to go and talk."

31

Patsy Ingle and I sat together under a street lamp on a park bench. Liesl and Melo had been scooped up into Fernando's cab, in spite of the fact that neither of them had wanted to leave.

"How did you—how did you come to know who I am?" Patsy asked.

"I was having tea with your mother, and she mentioned your nickname, Rainy-Day, so it was easy to put two and two together."

"You were having tea with my mother?" Patsy looked at me strangely. "How on earth did that come about?"

I licked my lips. How had all this happened? "I was looking for gold," I said finally.

"Gold?" she asked, a little startled.

"And I guess I look like you, when you were my age. I mean, she—well, she really wanted me to be you."

She stared hard at me and then put down her bags that she had been clutching to her chest. "I keep thinking I will go and see her, but I haven't yet been able to even let her know I've come home. How does she seem?"

"She misses you," I said.

Patsy looked startled again.

"She's building you a castle. And calling it Patsy's Castle."

Patsy groaned. "I don't want a castle."

"And all she wants before she dies is for you to know that she's never regretted anything so much as what she did to you and Leo. So I thought I should tell you. Because she's pretty old, and she might not be around much longer." A look of pain crossed Patsy's face. "Also, I met Leo, and he's really nice," I added in a rush.

Patsy smiled. "He *is* really nice," she agreed. After a moment she said, "She really said that? That she regrets—"

I nodded again.

"Mother changed so completely after my father died," she said after a moment. "Bertie and I were lucky that Rosie and Ernie Schwartz just plain adopted us, and Leo and Lizzie were so wonderful to grow up with. I remember the exact moment when I knew I loved Leo." Patsy laughed, pulling her hair back into a ponytail. Under the lamplight I thought she looked like a young girl.

Patsy paused for a moment. A group of teenagers were going by us on skateboards. She waited until they moved on.

"Mother, of course, was so furious when she finally opened her eyes. Bertie was upset with me, too, because he wanted me to stand up to her. He couldn't understand why I didn't just run off with Leo. I couldn't, you know, not at that time. Mother was—you can't imagine how fierce she was."

"I guess I can, actually," I said. "She's still pretty fierce."

Patsy put a hand on my arm. "I have to admit this to you, Aiden. I know now that I should have stood up to her.

But I think there was some part of me that *did* want to be a princess and grow up to live in a castle. Perhaps, I thought, in the end Leo wouldn't be able to provide for a princess." She sighed deeply. "And then Mother sent me to some silly school across the ocean in order to learn social graces!" She made a face. "I'm afraid I realized too late that I wasn't suited for the princess life." She made another face and then went on. "From time to time I'd hear from Rosie, and I always wrote her back. But then one day she wrote and said Mother had found one of my letters, and it would be better if we didn't communicate anymore. I thought maybe Rosie was just trying to protect me, put the past behind us and all that, especially as I found out from Bertie that Leo had a new girl-friend. So after I graduated from that awful school, I chose to stay away and not come home. I couldn't bear to come back, anyway, and find Leo married, with a swarm of children—"

"But he never married!" I said.

Patsy shook out her ponytail and then gathered her hair back into the rubber band. "Well, that makes two of us then!" She was quiet for a moment before she went on. "I drifted in Europe for a long time," she finally went on, "but then I decided to go to a veterinary school in England. Mother had sent Bertie away to a boarding school, too. She chose a school upstate, a school that was on a farm. Curiously enough our Grandpa James helped found it. He had grown up on a farm, and he believed kids should learn to use their hands as well as their heads and be close to the land. Well, as it turned out, Bertie loved the farming life!"

I shifted a bit on the park bench, thinking about Bertie Ingle, wondering what kind of farm he'd had.

"Honestly," said Patsy, "I think our farming ancestry must have run strongly in our blood—Bertie and I were so much happier being rugged in the country than in the life-style our mother wanted for us. I never, never would have been happy in a castle!" She seemed to think about this for some time, and then she went on, "Well, anyway, I started practicing raptor rehab in the English midlands and was very happy doing it. And then Bertie came for a visit. He had graduated from college and wanted to tell me he was getting married to a lovely girl who was as excited about farming as he was. They were going to buy their own farm."

As I sat there, I could feel my eyelids beginning to get heavy. It had been a long day.

But then Patsy sort of groaned. "It was during that visit that we had a fight," she said, her voice catching.

"Oh," I said, waking up a bit. Under the lamplight I could see Patsy's eyes filling with tears.

"He asked me again why I hadn't stood up to Mother, followed my heart, and married Leo. I admitted that I had been afraid, afraid that Mother would cut me off from my inheritance if I'd disobeyed her. That's when he told me he was disinheriting himself from the Ingle fortune. He said he was going to change his name so that he wouldn't have to carry the burden of being an Ingle for the rest of his life. Standing there, listening to him, I felt heartbroken all over again. Now, of course, he was a full-grown man with a dark beard coming in, broad shoulders, and a weathered look from being outside all day. But all I could do was picture the sweet little boy I had known, the little boy with the impish smile and the dimple on his chin."

I sat up. The portrait of Grandpa Farmer and the photograph I had seen on Patsy's girlhood dressing table came into focus.

"Well, Bertie went home, and I didn't hear from him

for a long time after that," said Patsy. "I wrote him letters, but they always came back. Address unknown. Many years went by. And then I got word, one day, from a lawyer, that Bertie and his wife had died in a car accident. He'd made some kind of arrangement that if he should die, we, Mother and I, would be notified; but that was all—no information beyond that. I called the attorney's office, but they told me they were very sorry there was nothing more they could tell me. I came home and hired an investigator. Let me tell you, there is a lot of farmland, and there are a lot of farms in this country. I wasn't even sure he was still upstate. I put an ad in the farming magazines. Turned up nothing. Bertie had hidden himself well."

My stomach was beginning to swirl, and I felt really dizzy. I pulled the gold watch out of my pocket. I pressed the knob and it flicked open. F.B. to E.I.

Patsy pulled at her ponytail again. She was quiet for a long time. "I just wish I knew," she said finally. "I just wish I knew what Bertie had changed his name to—I never knew if he had a family or anything."

My whole body was shaking. "I think it was Farmer," I said, gasping. "I think he changed his name to Farmer."

32

Mom was mad and upset with me for coming back late and not calling her. I told her I was sorry and went straight to bed. Lying on my back in that bed hanging from the ceiling in Tony's apartment, I stared up at the darkness, thinking more about Patsy and Bertie and Mrs. Ingle.

After I had showed Patsy the pocket watch and told her about the painting of my grandfather, Herb Farmer, she'd sat there for a long time, asking me a ton of questions. And then finally she said, "Herbert. That was Bertie's first name, so that makes sense. And then Farmer. Well, it figures he'd choose that as a last name. It fits his sense of humor." She smiled. "And now, well, now we know why you and I look alike."

Patsy accepted the whole idea so easily, but it seemed to me so hard to believe I didn't say a word about it to Mom. Patsy said she was going back to the lawyer who had handled Bertie's affairs to see if she could get proof, so there was nothing I could do but just wait and see.

There had been more, though, to Patsy's story. She told me how she had returned to England after not being able to turn up anything about her brother, and she thought she'd never come back home again. But just a year ago, she'd changed her mind. She said she felt the need to be close to Rosie and Ernie again and she knew her mother was old. She wanted to be certain, in spite of everything, that her mother was all right.

She came home and started working at the University of Gloria's raptor rehabilitation center, about a half an hour out of town, fixing up the injured birds that came her way. But she had not yet been able to bring herself to meet her mother face to face. And she hadn't let Rosie and Ernie know she was home, either. Instead, every two weeks or so, she'd come through the old secret passage that she and Bertie had discovered when they were kids.

Patsy had laughed, saying, "Of course it might not be a secret to the people who maintain the lampposts and the fountain and all the other things that require underground cables around here, but I'd say it's a secret to most people, and most people probably would think twice before wriggling through it. But not me, I like to. It makes me feel like a kid again."

Once she went through, Patsy changed her clothes and pretended to be a resident of the Ingle Building. She made her way up and down either Rosie or Ernie's elevator, asking questions, making sure Rosie and Ernie were all right, hearing, from time to time, things about Leo and his clock business. Of course she heard all about her mother, too, finding out that she was still going strong.

"I keep telling myself, okay, this is the day I'm going to say to Rosie and Ernie, It's me, Patsy. And every day I say to myself, this is the day I'm going to go up to the Eyrie and announce to my mother, I'm home."

"She's not so bad," I said. "You just have to look her in the eye and give it to her straight."

Patsy laughed. "Easy for you to say."

As I lay there in the dark, I got a picture in my mind of Patsy and Mrs. Ingle standing on separate chunks of rocky islands in a huge gray ocean. They couldn't get to each other and slowly the islands crumbled just like those sugar cubes that were in my tea.

I sat straight up in bed. Were Mom and I getting to be like Patsy and her mother? I scooched to the edge of my bed, feeling for the bookcase with my foot, and got myself down to the floor. I climbed into Mom's bed.

"Aiden?"

I didn't say a word. I just lay there and cuddled up against her. And then she didn't say anything more either, she just wrapped her arms around me.

Soon after that, Patsy Rain Ingle and I stood on the grass in the middle of Gill Park very early in the morning. She was wearing long black leather gloves, falconry gloves she called them. She was holding Lady Peregrine to her chest. The bird's eyes seemed huge, and she was panting with excitement. She began to thrash about.

"Yes, yes, Lady," said Patsy, "you're a feisty one, aren't you, and you're more than ready to fly back home."

Patsy held her out in front of her with outstretched arms. "One . . . two . . ." she counted, and on three she released the falcon. Lady Peregrine erked loudly and flew far across the lawn and landed in a tree in the Gill Park grove.

"She'll find her way after a bit," said Patsy. "Their internal navigational systems are flawless. She just has to get used to being outside again."

Patsy and I sat down on the grass to keep an eye on her. It had been a couple of really crazy days, and I was glad to be taking a break from everything.

Patsy had gone to Bertie's lawyer and told them what she suspected. Enough time had gone by since Bertie's death and they were able to go back into the records—and it all turned out to be true.

Herb Farmer, my grandfather, was one and the same person as Bertie Ingle. Patsy Ingle was my great-aunt. And Mrs. Ingle—Mrs. Ingle was my great-grandmother.

Patsy came over and met Mom and Tony. Mom kept saying, "I just can't believe it" over and over again.

"Is there any chance Pops knew?" I wanted to know.

Mom shook her head. "If Pops had known, I would have known. He wouldn't have kept something like that from me. But what a strange twist of fate, that I, a Balboni, should have ended up marrying an Ingle."

We asked Patsy millions of questions about Bertie. I think we wanted to know all the ways he and Pops might have been alike.

Sitting on the grass now, I had another question to ask Patsy.

"The story about looking for gold?" I asked. "The one you were telling Melo that day at the soccer game?"

"My father told us that story—I always thought it was about me—a little girl who goes looking for gold so she can build a castle—and it was connected to a treasure hunt he and your great-grandfather set up for us." Patsy laughed at the memory. "I think we were looking for something like Gold Falcons, those pretty old coins that aren't worth a whole lot. You know, I don't think we ever did find them."

I wanted to hear the rest of the story, but I checked

my pocket watch and saw it was time for me to go to the Ingle Building to meet Mrs. Ingle for the first time as her great-granddaughter. I scrambled to my feet.

Mrs. Ingle had been told everything—the Balboni connection as well—everything except that Patsy was home. Patsy wanted to be the one to tell her.

Fernando met me and took me in his taxi to the Ingle Building. I had told him and Ana everything, too. "*Opa! What a world this is!*" was all they'd said, and they'd laughed their heads off as if it was the funniest thing in the world.

My stomach was twinging like crazy as I rode up in number 10. Tony was at the controls, and he rested a big paw of a hand on my shoulder as we reached the top floor. "You okay, Aiden?"

I swallowed hard. "I just—it just feels so weird. I don't feel like an Ingle, and I don't think I ever will. And for all I know, Mrs. Ingle might not like me being an Ingle. She might think I'm after her fortune or something, which I'm not. I'd much rather be a Farmer than an Ingle."

"Once a Farmer, always a Farmer," said Tony with a smile. "By the way, Aiden, I have some news for you. Felix Brown told me he's been very worried about Charles, how he's been acting strange, running away all the time, and he finally figured out it's because he's been putting Charles under too much pressure. You can't be Best in Show *and* learn how to talk like a human. So Felix says he's just going to lay off on pushing the talking bit for a while. I'm very disappointed, actually. I was looking forward to having long conversations with Charles."

I couldn't help grinning, but I wondered if Felix still was going to look for the gold.

Ana met me at the door of the apartment. "She's ready

for you," she said, giving me an encouraging pat on the arm. I pulled at my blouse. I was wearing "the outfit."

Mrs. Ingle was wearing a cream-colored suit. Every one of her curls was tightly in place. She stared at me for what seemed like a hundred minutes. "Well!" she said finally. "I am told there is a reason why you so resemble my daughter."

I didn't know what to say. I felt shy and tongue-tied.

"I'm going up to the Eyrie now, Ana, and this young lady will join me—and no, not you, Ana, just the two of us."

Ana helped Mrs. Ingle into a warm jacket, and in a moment we were in front of the industrial elevator. I opened the door and we went in. Mrs. Ingle pressed a button and, with a slight buzzing, the elevator began to rise slowly. Mrs. Ingle didn't say a word as we went up. We came to a stop near the top and, as we stepped through the door, we were outside, jillions of feet high, on a deck with a high railing that seemed to circle the mountain. And right in the middle was the giant gold falcon. It took my breath away.

The gold talons of the falcon were big and curved and scary-looking: They could have picked up a taxi, no problem, and you could also see scales and ridges on them, and on the legs, too. There were layers and layers of feathers on the falcon's breast and the big, tapered flight feathers on the wings. I tipped my head back to look up at the head, but it was all too dazzling to see.

It was one thing to look up; it was another to look down. Out there was the city of Gloria where little windows everywhere shimmered in the sunlight.

Mrs. Ingle lifted a trembling hand and pointed, "Over there is the ledge where the Lord and Lady have made their home."

We walked a few feet, and there was a sort of box built

from scraps of wood resting on the edge of the deck. "They don't nest like eagles," she said. "They just like to have a little shelter. I was hoping they'd produce chicks this year—but I'm afraid the Lady has been injured. I've left countless messages for the Bird Lady, but she won't return my calls."

Mrs. Ingle seemed very shaky. Watching her, I was scared she might fall or faint. "There's a bench right here, Mrs. Ingle. Let's sit down for a bit." She clutched my arm and held on to me as we sat.

"Thank you," she said, "you're a strong, sturdy girl, Aiden. It must be your farming background. Now, I want you tell me about yourself and what brought you here to the Ingle Building and into my life. I want to hear everything."

And so for the next little while, I found myself telling her all about the dairy farm and all about Pops and about Mom and me trying to make a go of it and then having to put the farm up for sale and moving to Gloria because Mom had grown up here. I told her about living with Tony in his tiny apartment and how hard it was to go to a new school where I was the only new girl in the class. Then I told her how I'd found a clue in my great-grandfather Balboni's hat right about the same time I learned about the lost treasure. I broke off for a moment as I realized that in the end the hat had probably belonged to Edward Ingle!

"And then," I said finally, "I thought if I could find the Gold Falcons, I'd be able to buy back my farm."

She looked at me with interest. "And have you found the Falcons?"

"No," I said, "and I figured out at some point that even if I had I wouldn't be allowed to keep them."

Mrs. Ingle didn't comment. She shut her eyes and sat there without speaking for a long time, then opened them.

"You didn't find the gold, but in the process I found you," she said finally. "I would say that I am the lucky one; I'm really the one who found the treasure." She took my hand in hers. "I would like," she said, "to ask one thing of you." I waited, trying to imagine what it could possibly be. "I would like for you to take me to see your farm, the place where Bertie made his home."

And it was in that moment, just off in the distance, that we saw two black shapes silhouetted against the blue sky. Mrs. Ingle sat up, shading her eyes with her hands. They came closer and closer, two falcons, flying side by side, the black patches around their eyes and their black-and-white speckled markings showing up more and more clearly as they approached.

They landed on the ledge right in front of us.

Mrs. Ingle put back her head and laughed a hearty, out-loud laugh, not a tinkly icicle laugh at all. It was if something inside her had melted.

When we got back down to the apartment, Ana took me aside. "Patsy will be here in an hour," she said with shining eyes.

Both Mom and I had stayed home from school for a few days, talking to Patsy, trying to take in the strange idea that Grandpa Farmer had started out in life being an Ingle. But then Mom had said, "I don't care if your ancestors turn out to be the kings and queens of England, Aiden, you can't miss another day of school."

It was strange walking down the hallway of the East Park Day School, knowing that my great-great-grandfather, James Ingle, had owned this building once. As I was hanging up my coat in the locker room, I heard Marisa talking to Asha a few lockers down.

"I'm *not* leaving you out, Asha. Quentin and I aren't even *looking* anymore. Madame Petrovna told us not to. And I don't know if this means she's not going to help me get into the ballet school anymore. Everything's terrible, so just stop thinking about yourself for five minutes, okay?"

I walked with Adam into homeroom. "So, where have you been? Were you out sick? When are we going back to the Ingle Building?"

I was in the middle of telling him that Felix Brown wasn't looking for gold anymore when Marisa came up to us. "Oh,

Farmer Girl," she said, "I thought maybe you weren't coming back to school, but here you are. Have you been out milking the cows?"

I turned and looked at her. "Actually I'm *Aiden.* Farmer Girl is my twin." Marisa looked at me strangely. "So if you call me Farmer Girl, I might not answer. I know I look just like her, but she's sick today so I came in so her attendance record wouldn't get messed up. Don't tell anyone, though, okay?"

Marisa turned red, but she didn't say another word. At recess, she was standing near me when Gareth Pugh came up and invited me to play baseball. Her mouth dropped open.

After school, I met Fernando for a soccer lesson. "Start thinking with your feet, Aiden, not with your head," he said. At soccer practice the next day, I actually got hold of the ball and tried out the kick Fernando had taught me. It worked. The ball sailed in a curvy arc right into the net.

The next day, as I was walking through Gill Park on my way home, I ran into a swarm of gorillas. Gareth Pugh was standing in the middle of them, wearing his baseball cap and punching his fist into his baseball glove. He suddenly spotted me and grabbed me by the arm. "Can you play?" he asked. "We're down a player."

As I was struggling to put on a gorilla suit, for one heart-stopping moment I thought I saw Marisa coming toward me. "Welcome to the team!" she said. I realized with relief that it was Frankie. "Hey, Aiden Farmer, you're on our team. Awesome," Liesl said as she came over and started punching me.

The gorilla suit felt warm and cozy. The air felt fresh against my face. Gill Park music drifted down with the falling leaves. Right now, at this moment, the city seemed pretty good. And the Gorillas won the game.

Over all, it was a pretty great week, although I kept putting off telling Liesl and Adam I was an Ingle. I needed to find the right moment. They kept bugging me to get back to the Ingle Building, and Liesl wasn't reassured when I told her that Marisa and Quentin weren't looking for the Gold Falcons anymore. She was sure someone with the metal detectors would find them.

"Saturday," I finally told them, "I'll meet you on the rooftop of the east wing." My plan was to tell them the whole Ingle-Farmer story up there. But first, I wanted some time with Rosie Schwartz alone.

As the doors to Rosie's elevator opened, Rosie took one look at me and rushed to give me an enormous hug. Then she held me at arm's length, her face beaming. "Aiden! You've brought Patsy back into our lives! She came to see us yesterday. And then she told us everything—oh, dolling, who would have ever guessed that your mother, a Balboni, should end up with an Ingle?"

"Not really an Ingle," I said, feeling a little grumpy about this. "A Farmer."

"Of course, Aiden, of course," said Rosie soothingly. She sat on the stool, clucking at me like an old hen. I had never seen her more cheerful.

"Rosie, can you tell me what that key was for that you asked me to give Ernie?"

"Well!" Rosie exclaimed. She looked at me for a long minute and seemed to make up her mind. "Why don't you sit down in that chair, Aiden. You might feel more comfortable hearing this sitting down. You being like a part of the family and all, I'm going to tell you the whole story." She closed the doors to the elevator and waited for me to sit down. And then she said, "Before he died, Edward Ingle gave Ernie and me ten Gold Falcons."

I couldn't help gasping a bit, and Rosie nodded. "I knew you were better off sitting down." She shifted on her stool and leaned toward me. "Mr. Ingle fully believed that one day the Gold Falcons would be worth something again, and he wanted us to have them. And then he and Mr. Balboni hid that other 10—expecting, I'm sure, the children would find them, but never intending to give them away. They would have substituted chocolate gold coins or some such thing as a prize, I'm sure. But, as you know, Mr. Ingle died, and those Gold Falcons were never found."

Someone called for the elevator, but Rosie paid no attention.

"Now, Ernie and I kept our Gold Falcons in our house for years and years," she went on. "On a shelf in the kitchen alongside the cookbooks, if you can believe that." She laughed, shaking her head. "But after all, for years they were worth about as much as the buttons on this jacket. Then comes the day all these years later when the coins have come to be worth something. A whole bundle more than we ever dreamed." Rosie shook her head again. "Well, Ernie and I knew we had to get the Falcons out of the house. Over the years, too many folks had heard us talk about them. 'Let's put 'em in the bank,' I said. 'No banks,' said Ernie. 'Newspapers will get wind of it, and there will be no end of nonsense.' He gets it into his head to hide the gold at the feet of the gold falcon. 'We'll put gold where gold is,' he said, 'and no one will think of looking for it there.' Besides, he reasoned, no one goes up there except for him and Mrs. Ingle—him to change the bulbs in the lamps now and then and she to dote on her birds. Okay with all this, Aiden? Are you following?"

I nodded. I was still amazed that Rosie and Ernie had had 10 Gold Falcons of their own all this time.

Rosie took a breath. "But then, right about when the news broke about the Falcons being worth something, Ernie began to notice Grip was paying extra-special attention to him. 'He's after our gold, Rosie. He thinks if he follows me around, he'll find 'em.' Then we heard through the grapevine—believe me, Aiden, having all our relatives working here means there aren't too many secrets—that Mrs. Ingle told Grip she'd give him a reward if he could find those lost Gold Falcons for her."

"Ooh," I couldn't help saying. So much was becoming clear to me now.

"Well now," Rosie continued, "there's not a square inch of this building that Ernie doesn't know. He knows there's a space in the walls underneath the mountain, a sort of well. He knows there's a ladder that goes up the well. Cutting an opening right behind the clock, he crawls through it and goes up that ladder from the bottom of the well to the bottom of the industrial elevator. That's the elevator that goes up inside the mountain—don't know if you can picture such a thing."

"Yes, I can," I said, smiling a bit.

"Well, good," said Rosie, beaming. "So Ernie cuts another opening in the bottom of the industrial elevator so he can let himself in there without a soul knowing what he's up to. He's not a young man anymore to be crawling through this and that and climbing up ladders, but I honestly think a part of him liked the adventure of it!" She laughed fondly, shaking her head a bit.

The call for the elevator came again. "Okay, okay, hold your horses, be there in a jiffy," said Rosie, waving a hand impatiently. She leaned back, continuing, "Then comes the day Grip boots Ernie out of number 10—you were here with me, dolling, when that happened, and I don't mind telling you I was mad as a hornet. All I could think of at the time was that it was time to let go of this building. Good riddance and all that. We have those Falcons, so we're free. Mrs. Ingle, she doesn't seem to need us anymore, and Ernie and me, we're not getting any younger, and there's a few places we'd like to go besides trundling up and down these elevators all the livelong day.

"So one evening, behind the clock Ernie goes, but Grip's been lurking around spying as usual, and Ernie's all nervous; he drops the key somewhere inside that well. So then what? He takes it into his head to climb up the *outside* of the mountain to get at the gold. There's these iron rungs bolted right into the granite. There was a time when Ernie prided himself on being able to climb up there. But that was a hundred years ago, dolling, when he was as spry as a monkey. Now, I'm telling you, he's about as spry as an old *donkey* and just as stubborn to boot. He waits till it's dark, so he can climb up without anyone seeing him. Of course, I don't know a thing about this." Rosie held her hands to her heart. "Oh, my! When I think of how he might have been hurt!"

There was a series of *bings*. "Oh dolling, I better get a move on," said Rosie, making a face. "There's not much more to tell. I'll finish up when you come back down."

As soon as I came out onto the rooftop terrace, I looked up at the gold falcon. Rosie hadn't said whether or not Ernie had collected their ten Gold Falcons. Maybe they were still up there. And maybe the other half of the Gold Falcons was up there, too.

THE BIRD OF TIME HAS NOT FAR TO FLY.

I should have paid more attention when I was up there with Mrs. Ingle.

I looked around for Liesl and Adam, and then my heart almost stopped. Grip was standing in the middle of the terrace. He didn't see me because he was staring up at the gold falcon, too. He was holding my hat in his hand. I couldn't help myself. I ran toward Grip yelling, "That's my hat, give it back to me."

Grip whirled on me. "You! I'm not giving you back nothin', little lady, not until I get some information out of you." He pulled out a phone. "This time I'm calling security, and you're not leaving until you talk!"

Out of the corner of my eye, I saw Felix Brown. He'd been standing at the railing, Charles was perched on his shoulder. As he heard Grip's raised voice, he came over to us, looking concerned.

"I have good reason to believe you got your hands on some Gold Falcons what don't belong to you," said Grip.

"I don't," I said. "I—" But then I froze, unable to say another word. Plummeting straight down out of the sky at a hundred miles per hour was a peregrine falcon. It was heading with an outstretched foot straight for Charles.

"Watch out!" I screamed.

Just as Charles was gripped in the falcon's talons, a tub of flowers came sailing through the air—flowers, falcon, and Charles all hung in space for a frozen second—and then the falcon veered off sharply, dropping Charles as the tub of flowers landed full in Grip's face. Grip fell over backward with a crash, while Felix crouched, cowering, his arms crossed over his head.

People seemed to appear from everywhere. Two men in jackets marked security strode right by me and over to Grip. And then I noticed Adam and Liesl were standing behind right me. Adam was tufting up his hair with both hands, and Liesl, her eyes huge, had one hand planted over her mouth.

"What happened here?" one of the security men was asking.

"That bird came diving down, and someone threw that tub of flowers at it," a man said. "Guess they meant to hit the bird, but they missed."

Adam, Liesl, and I pressed forward a bit closer. Grip was sitting up, but groaning and moaning, holding his jaw. Felix was on his hands and knees calling frantically for Charles.

"I'm outta here," said Liesl, pulling me by the arm. "Places to go, people to meet."

We were halfway down the hall when I said, "Where's Adam? Where'd he go?"

Liesl kept pulling me. "Come on, keep going. Can't wait for him."

Rosie's elevator appeared, and Adam finally came racing down the hall. He leaped into the elevator just as the doors were closing.

"Adam, where were you?"

"Just getting something," he said. He held out my hat.

"Adam!" I couldn't believe it. I took the hat from him and pressed it against my face. "I never thought I'd see it again. Thanks!"

"Holy mouse tails, Liesl," he said, "what were you thinking, hurling that thing like that?"

"I had to save Charles," she said.

"*You* threw that?" I asked, turning to Liesl.

"I have a good arm," she said proudly. "Gareth Pugh can tell you what a good arm I have."

"Yeah, a good arm," said Adam. "But terrible aim."

"I'm *glad* it didn't hit the falcon," said Liesl.

I turned to Rosie and explained. "Grip was up there, and he got knocked down flat by a tub of flowers."

"Oh my," said Rosie, the corners of her mouth tugging up. "I'm so sorry to hear that."

As we were leaving the elevator, I hung back a moment. "Rosie, did you ever get the Gold Falcons?"

"Yes, we did," said Rosie. "We couldn't risk letting them sit around. Who knows, Lord Peregrine might have gone off with them and built himself a fancy condo. Can't trust anyone these days." She chuckled to herself.

"Does Leo know about all of this?" I asked.

"Yes, of course, dolling!" said Rosie. "Most naturally he is included in our good fortune, and so is Lizzie. And so are my brothers and sisters, Stan, Marty, Adele, Dorota, and Boris."

"And Stefan," I said.

"Oh good heavens!" Rosie said. "I'm always forgetting Stefan!"

"And are you and Ernie going to retire?" The thought of the Ingle Building without Rosie and Ernie made me sad.

"Not quite yet, dolling. I believe Grip is losing his grip. Soon as Ernie's mended, he's going to be reinstalled in number 10. Oh, the two of us, we just wouldn't know what to do with ourselves if we didn't have our ups and downs!"

Fernando was driving Mrs. Ingle's fancy car, and Mrs. Ingle was sitting beside him in the front seat. Mom, Ana, and I were in the backseat. Never, in a million years, did I think the next time I saw the farm it would be with Mrs. Ingle.

Mrs. Ingle napped almost all of the way. Ana told me that all the events of the last week had exhausted her.

My heart began bumping with excitement as things started to get familiar. There was the Stanley horse farm and the Miller family gas station and general store and the elementary school. Soon we were passing Blake's farm—the big red barn was freshly painted and the silo stood up tall and proud.

And now we were driving up our road, with the stone walls and maple trees on either side, and now here we were in front of our big white house with the sagging porch. The hay barn was across the driveway and the cow barn was set back a way. It was strange to see the FOR SALE sign planted in the lawn, and it was way too quiet without Nellie and Hector running out to greet us.

Ana and Fernando helped Mrs. Ingle out of the car while I ran up the front porch steps. Mom had the key, and I thought she'd never get the door open. Inside, the house smelled different, damp and mildewy, like a house that missed its people. I ran into the kitchen and quickly, before anyone could see me, threw my arms around the big post in the middle and said, "I'm back."

"Make a fire, why don't you," said Mom, coming in. "Take the chill off and Mrs. Ingle can warm herself in here."

In a flash, I was out the backdoor and stood filling my lungs with the tang of fallen leaves and apples and wild grapes. I loaded up my arms with logs, loving the scratchy feel of the bark beneath my chin. Coming back into the kitchen, I scrunched up a wad of newspaper and stuck it in the woodstove with some kindling and a few logs. That first whiff of woodsmoke was like perfume.

"Show me the portrait, Aiden," said Mrs. Ingle. She was standing in the kitchen looking out of place.

I took her hand, so dry and whispery-feeling, and led her to the living room. The old painting was on the back wall. Beside it was the old grandfather clock. "Oh!" we both exclaimed at the same time. Mrs. Ingle was looking at the painting, but I was looking at the clock. She took a step toward the painting, while I just stood still and stared. The head of a falcon was directly above the number 12 on the dial, its wings curving down on either side, forming a frame.

"THE BIRD OF TIME HAS NOT FAR TO FLY," I said out loud.

"Can you take the painting off the wall?" Mrs. Ingle asked.

Fernando, who had come in, strode across the room. The painting had the same feeling to it as Mrs. Ingle's portrait, the same sort of brushstrokes, but yellows and browns instead of pink. And what a cute boy Bertie had been, with his smile and his dimple. Fernando carefully lifted the painting off the wall.

"Let me see the back," said Mrs. Ingle.

Ana, who was there, too, pulled out a tissue from her bag and ran it around the frame. A lot of dust had collected. Fernando turned the painting and on the back of the canvas the name Herbert James Farmer was written on a piece of white tape.

"And get that tape off, will you?" Mrs. Ingle said.

Fernando pulled out a pocketknife. Very carefully, he poked the tip of the knife under one end of the tape. It came off without any trouble at all.

Herbert James Ingle. There it was, as clear as day.

"Well!" said Mrs. Ingle. She sank into a couch.

And then moving in a sort of trance, I stepped toward the clock.

"And unless I'm terribly mistaken that is the clock that used to stand in our dining room in the Eyrie," said Mrs. Ingle. "Bertie took it with him when he left."

I reached for a little door in the side of the clock at the top. I realized I didn't even need to stand on tiptoes to do this anymore. The little door slid open, and I poked my arm in all the way to the back. Nothing. No, I thought, that would have been too easy. Edward Ingle liked a bit more of a challenge. Dropping to the floor, I looked along the bottom edge at the base of the clock. In the back there was a panel, slightly lighter in color, that I'd never noticed before. It slid to one side. Sitting inside was a wooden box. I pulled it out, feeling the weight of it. It was plenty heavy. Ten Gold Falcons *would* be heavy.

"What have you got there, Aiden?" asked Fernando.

I sat back on my heels and without opening the box, I said, "Oh, just Things."

Mrs. Ingle said she was ready for a nap. I took her up to Mom's bedroom and then while Mom and Ana cooked supper, I showed Fernando around.

"It is like the farm Ana and I always dream of," Fernando said, as we stood in the hay barn. Swallows flew in and out of the eaves. He sighed. "And the dream will come true, some day, as long as *Senhora* Formiga and I keep working!"

We ate in the kitchen where it was warm, around the old kitchen table, and then, after washing up, it was time to go. As Mrs. Ingle was being helped out to the car, I quickly ran up to my bedroom. I lay down on my bed and looked out the window. The evening star hung in the upper righthand corner. "I'll be back," I promised it.

But as we were driving back to Gloria through the dark, Mrs. Ingle suddenly turned in her seat, and she said, "Aiden Farmer Ingle, I would like you and your mother to come live with me in the Eyrie."

I felt Mom reach for my hand. Neither of us said anything for a moment, and then Mom, clearing her throat, said, "That's a very nice offer, Mrs. Ingle. We will certainly consider it."

It was Sunday, so Leo wasn't working at his shop. I asked him to meet me in Ana's garden in the park. I ran as fast as I could to get there. I could hardly stand holding on to the secret of the Gold Falcons one moment longer, but I was afraid to tell anyone about them until I had talked to him.

Leo arrived wearing a brown leather jacket. There was something different about him. He seemed younger.

"You!" he said, his whole face crinkling.

"Me?"

He threw his arms around me in a bear hug and nearly squeezed the life out of me. Then he held me at arm's length and just stared at me for a minute. "Aiden Farmer Ingle," he said finally, "thank you for bringing back my girl."

I swallowed hard and looked away. There were tears in Leo's eyes.

"Now then, Aiden. You called *me*. What's on your mind?"

"Can we sit down?" I tugged him over to a bench.

Shivering slightly, I sat down, and Leo pulled the jacket more tightly around him. The air felt like winter was coming pretty soon. Across the way, I saw Old Violet sitting on a bench. I hoped she was warm enough.

"Leo, I want to talk to you about Gold Falcons."

Leo sat up. "Yes?"

"Rosie told me about the ones Edward Ingle gave her and Ernie."

"Yes," said Leo. "Amazing good fortune, especially as it now appears that Pa is going to live to enjoy it."

"It was half of the collection."

"Yes," said Leo.

I cleared my throat. "I found the other half."

Leo's eyes widened. "Did you?"

"In the grandfather clock at home—in the farmhouse."

Leo let out a long breath. "Ahhh," he said, his eyes crinkling, "finally."

"Finally?" I jumped off the bench. "You *knew*?" I was shouting, and a flock of pigeons that had been scratching at the ground near us rose up in a flutter.

Leo grabbed my hand and made me sit back down on the bench. "Not always! Not by a long shot! I've been slow to see what's been under my nose ever since I met you and your hat and your pocket watch. But my brain cells began to wake up right around the time you made the observation that all the clues had to do with birds or time. And I began to wonder, how *do* those things fit together? Well, the pocket watch certainly fit those two categories—the falcon on it, and it being a timepiece—but obviously it was too small to be a hiding place for Gold Falcons. Being a man who works with clocks, I gradually got to thinking of a clock I had remembered as a child—a grandfather clock with a falcon painted on the dial. Now where *was* that clock, I wondered. It had been up in the Eyrie, but then I remembered—Bertie carried it away with him when he left. Presumably it was in his farmhouse, wherever that was."

Leo brushed back a lock of white hair that had fallen over his eyes. "There were a lot of little nudges, little hints. Birds and time, and then, *bam*, there was that moment in Pa's elevator when Mrs. Ingle called you Patsy. I stared at you, and then I saw it—the resemblance. The nudges turned into a great big hammer hitting me over the head. You looked like Patsy Ingle, you had mentioned a grandfather clock with a falcon on it the very first moment I met you, and you had that pocket watch, the biggest clue of all: *From F.B. to E.I.* There was the proof of your heritage, Aiden, staring us in the face, not to mention the name 'Farmer.' Bertie had a sense of humor, all right. But the Balboni connection confused everything. Well, standing there in the elevator, I wasn't about to blurt out I thought you were Bertie Ingle's granddaughter. I quick came up with a clue I hoped might nudge *you* in the right direction."

"*You* wrote that clue," I said, turning red as I remembered how Adam and I had suspected *Leo* of going off with the Gold Falcons. "TIME IS IN MY POCKET." I pulled the watch out.

Leo looked thoughtful. "I wasn't, of course, completely, 100 percent sure, you know, and there was, after all, the thrill of the hunt! I thought it best for you to make your own discoveries." He was crinkling again. "In any case, it has all come out just as I hoped it would. And better. Much, much better."

Black Jack and Henrietta suddenly appeared, weaving between our ankles. Leo bent down to give each one a pat.

"Leo," I said, "what should I do with the Gold Falcons?"

"First thing," said Leo, "is take them to the bank. Do not even *think* about hiding them at the top of the Ingle Building mountain." He shivered slightly, probably at the thought of Ernie pulling himself up those iron rungs. "Get 'em certified, or whatever it is they do to make sure they're the real thing. And then—"

"I'll have to tell Mrs. Ingle," I said.

"Yes, I expect that's true," said Leo.

I shifted on the bench a little. "Leo, there's another thing—you must have known I would never be able to keep the Gold Falcons if I found them. Why did you encourage me to go after them?"

Leo rubbed his chin. "The truth is, Aiden, even with that clue, I never thought in a million years that you *would* actually find them. I mean, no one ever had after all these years. But I thought a treasure hunt would be—I don't know—fun and distract you and help you forget how much you missed your home. And then, when you actually began to make progress, why then I very much believed that if you *did* find them Mrs. Ingle would reward you." He paused a moment, putting a hand on my shoulder. "And I sincerely hope that she does."

After Mom recovered from the first shock of seeing the Gold Falcons, we took them to a bank on Monday morning. The bank certified that they were real, all right, and in as perfect shape as the day they had been minted.

And then, I had the job of telling Mrs. Ingle about the Falcons. As I sat beside her on her poofy couch, it took her a while to take in the fact that I had actually found them in the grandfather clock in our living room at the farmhouse. She wanted me to explain all the clues to the treasure hunt over and over again. And then, feeling a lump in my throat, because after everything there was nothing I could do anymore to save the grove in Gill Park, I said, "And now you can build Patsy's Castle."

Mrs. Ingle sat, turning and twisting the rings on her fingers for a long time. Finally she said, "No, Aiden, they are not meant for me. I have no need for them and no need, either, to build Patsy a castle. She doesn't want one in any case. You found them and as they say, finder's keepers."

It was quiet in the Eyrie as I tried to take this in. Then she said, "I expect you and your mother will be going back to your farm." She looked so sad I could hardly bear to look at her, and a wave of confusing feelings swirled over me.

The very first thing Mom *did* do was take the farmhouse off the market. "You can go back to the country and live with Blake's family for the rest of the year if you want," she said. "And then I can join you by summertime. But I need to finish up the year here, Aiden, you can understand that, can't you? I can't just walk out on the school."

I swallowed hard. I knew how hard it was for Mom to consider going back to her old life. I didn't know if I could leave Gloria right now myself. I'd told Gareth Pugh I'd play the last Gorillas game of the season, and I was taking those soccer lessons from Fernando.

"And you should begin to do some thinking, Aiden, about what else you might want to do with the gold," said Mom.

I swallowed hard again. This was going to be way more difficult than I had ever imagined.

I left Tony's apartment and walked through the park until I came to Ana's garden. I was meeting Liesl and Adam because it finally was time to tell them about being an Ingle and about finding the gold. Old Violet was in the garden, too. "Where's your hat?" she screeched at me.

"No hat," I said. It was under my pillow, where I slept with it now instead of wearing it.

"No hat, no hat, only cats!" Old Violet screeched as Black Jack and Henrietta bounded through a hole in a hedge. I thought of how far Henrietta had come from that first day in the park when she'd hissed and spat at Jack.

"What," I asked the cats, "should I do?" Jack and Henrietta twitched their ears.

"Move back to the farm, like Mom said? But Mom wants

to be here, and I can't go without her. I'd miss her too much, and she'd miss me. And then there's Mrs. Ingle. I'm not sure it's such a good idea to leave her right now, even with Patsy back home 'cause Patsy is kind of spending a lot of time with Leo. And I know how to make her laugh, which Patsy can't do yet. And if Mom and I live up there with her in the Eyrie, we'd be so high up, Henrietta, like in a tree house, looking out over the whole world and we'd get to see Rosie every single day. And then there's school. I know East Park Day is a better school than the school at home, even though the kids at home are much nicer. Not really, though. It just takes time to get to know new people. Besides, I am doing better and better in school. I even beat Adam on the last vocabulary quiz."

"Hey!" said Adam, coming around the corner. "Are you talking to yourself?"

"Nope, to the cats," I said.

"Did I hear you saying something about beating me on a quiz?"

"Well, I did."

"Never again," he said, tufting up his hair.

Liesl arrived a minute later. She was crackling with anger. "Did you hear the news?" she said, almost spitting. "The Ingle Building Gold Falcons have been found. Can you believe that? They're not saying who found them, but that means it's all over. I have no idea where Mitch Bloom and I are going to live now."

"Sit down and be quiet for a minute, Liesl," I said. "I have some news for you, too, but I'm only going to tell you on one condition." She raised her eyebrows at me. "If you like what I tell you, you have to invite Adam up into the tree house."

"You *better* like it," said Adam.

And then I told them everything, and Liesl and Adam, after they got over the shock, both liked what I told them. "You're an Ingle," Liesl said, shaking her head. "Well, that means *I'm* an Ingle because I'm your cousin."

We started running and leaping through Gill Park, heading for the tree house. And we were standing beneath it, waiting for the elevator to come down, when someone started playing "Here Comes the Sun," into the park on the piano. A little kid started singing along with it, his voice high and sweet and perfect. My heart flipped over, and all three of us yelled "Melo!" at the same time.

Adam, Liesl, and I went up into the tree house and spent the rest of the afternoon there. We even got Adam to climb out a window and scramble onto a branch. I figured we'd get him comfortable climbing trees in about another month. And then, before we knew it, it was time to get ready for the opera.

Mrs. Ingle, Merla, Mom, Mitch, Liesl, Adam, and I all squeezed into Mrs. Ingle's box in the Ingle Building Opera House.

Down below, toward the front, I could see Leo and Patsy. Their two white heads were together, and they were laughing. Fernando and Ana and Melo were down below us, too. Melo looked up suddenly and started waving like crazy.

A man came out on the stage and everyone was quiet. "Ladies and gentlemen, we are pleased to announce the return of Antonio Balboni this evening in the role of Figaro."

There was a huge wave of clapping from the audience, and then the orchestra struck up the overture. When the curtain came up and everyone clapped for Tony again, Mom took my hand and squeezed it. Tony was doing great. His voice soared, and I thought of how he had told me, just that morning, that any time he started to panic he was going to imagine that we were in that well inside the Ingle Building and that he needed to sing to keep our spirits up.

Tony finished his song, and the audience adored him. Then I spotted Felix Brown in the middle of the first row. He was sitting next to Madame Petrovna. I nudged Adam and pointed. "There's Felix," I whispered.

"Yeah," he whispered back, "and I'm pretty sure Charles is on his shoulder."

I took Mom's opera glasses from her.

"It *is* Charles," I whispered. "And his mouth is open and he's singing along."

After the last Bravo! everyone went backstage. Mrs. Ingle shook Tony's hand and told him it was the very best performance she had heard and that she sincerely hoped he wasn't planning on giving up his singing career for elevator operating. "Because you're not so very good at *that*," she said.

Felix Brown and Charles had come backstage, too. Charles leaped right onto Tony's shoulder.

"If Charles could speak," said Felix, "I know he would say you were magnificent!"

"Perrrrfection," said Madame Petrovna.

And then Tony suggested we all go up to the rooftop to see the city of Gloria at night. Ana and Fernando, carrying a sleepy Melo between them, led the way to Rosie's elevator.

"Dollings!" Rosie exclaimed, beaming as we all trooped in. "All my favorite people!"

"Rooftop, Rosie!" Tony sang out at the top of his lungs.

He woke up Melo, who, staring at Patsy, suddenly said, "Bird Lady! Story! Tell the gold story!"

Patsy said, "Come, Melo, sit." She sat down on the chair and patted her knee and Melo climbed into her lap.

"From the beginning," he said.

Patsy was quiet a moment, and then she took a breath and began. "Once," she said, "there was a girl." She looked fondly at me and then went on. As she came to the number of steps the girl climbed, Melo giggled, but Adam and Liesl gave me such terrible looks they beat Marisa's *Look* hands down.

And then, finally, Patsy got to the part Melo and I hadn't heard yet.

"'Ma and Pa,' the girl called as she came to the top of her hill. 'Ma and Pa, come see what I have found!' She pulled the nuggets out of her pockets and held them up for her mother and father to see. But all they were now were rocks—dull, ordinary, cold, gray rocks, not shiny gold at all.

"'Oh, poor child, that is not gold!' And one by one, the girl sadly let the rocks fall to the ground.

"But then it seemed to her as if the grass said, 'Sow the rocks.'

"And it seemed as if the ants said, 'Dig the earth.'

"And she was sure that the clouds said, 'Let the rocks grow.'

"So the girl took a hoe and scraped the earth and one by one planted the rocks. And as she and her mother and father stood there, little shoots poked through the earth, and five trees grew up, tall and straight, right in front of their eyes. The first tree grew loaves of bread; the second grew chickens; the third grew a milk cow; the fourth, songbirds to roost in the trees; and the fifth?

"The fifth rock grew into a falcon.

"'All we really have,' said the falcon looking the girl in the eye, 'is—'"

Patsy suddenly broke off telling the story. "The ending

the way Pa told it isn't quite right," she said. "I have a new ending."

She took a deep breath. "'All,' said the falcon looking the girl in the eye, 'we really have is *love*.'

"And the bird spread its wings and flew away."

No one said anything for a minute. Melo just sat there, and you could almost see the thinking going on inside his eyes. "Is it a true story?" he finally asked.

"All stories are true," said Patsy with a smile.

And then Rosie said, "Rooftop! You have reached your destination!"

Mom and I held hands as we walked across the terrace over to the railing. We stood side by side looking out over the city of Gloria. Everywhere there were lights, except for the dark patch in the middle that was the park.

"I'm going to give some gold to Willy Wilson," I said suddenly, turning to Mom. "So Gill Park won't ever have to cut down its trees."

And as I saw Tony standing there with his arm around Merla, I said, "And some to Tony, so he can pay back his opera school debts."

And then I saw Fernando and Ana with Melo between them. "And Ana and Fernando and Melo can live at the farm and take care of it, and then you and I, Mom, can live in Gloria with Mrs. Ingle in the winter, and then go back home in the summer—or I can, if you don't want to."

Mom didn't say anything, but she put her arm around me and held me tight.

Then I looked up at the Eyrie, and while I couldn't see them I knew Lord and Lady Peregrine were settling in for the evening.